Spinners

William K. Durr
Jean M. LePere
John J. Pikulski
Ruth Hayek Brown

Consultant:
Hugh Schoephoerster

HOUGHTON MIFFLIN COMPANY   BOSTON

Atlanta   Dallas   Geneva, Illinois   Hopewell, New Jersey   Palo Alto   Toronto

Acknowledgments

Grateful acknowledgment is given for the contributions of Paul McKee.

For each of the selections listed below, grateful acknowledgment is made for permission to adapt and/or reprint copyrighted material, as follows:

"Anansi the African Spider," from *Plays from Folktales of Africa and Asia,* by Barbara Winther. Copyright © 1975 by Plays, Inc., and reprinted with their permission.

"Autumn Leaves," from *In the Woods, In the Meadow, In the Sky,* by Aileen Fisher. Published by Charles Scribner's Sons in 1965. Reprinted by permission of the author.

"The Beautiful," from *Folk Sayings from the Hawaiian.* Privately printed, Honolulu, 1961. Copyright by Jane Lathrop Winne with Mary Kawena Pukiu, Hawaiana Consultant. Reprinted by permission of the Bernice P. Bishop Museum.

"Blue-Wings-Flying," adapted from *Blue-Wings-Flying,* by Elizabeth Willis De Huff. Copyright © 1977 by Elizabeth Willis De Huff. Used by permission of Addison-Wesley Publishing Company, Inc.

"A Bowl of Sun," adapted from *A Bowl of Sun,* by Frances Wosmek. Used by permission of the publishers, Childrens Press.

"The Bridge," from *I Thought I Heard the City,* by Lilian Moore. Text copyright © 1969 by Lilian Moore. Used by permission of Atheneum Publishers.

"Bus Ride," adapted text of *Bus Ride,* by Nancy Jewell. Text copyright © 1978 by Nancy Bronson Jewell. Used by permission of Harper & Row, Publishers, Inc.

"Don't Ever Cross a Crocodile," from *Don't Ever Cross a Crocodile,* by Kaye Starbird. Copyright © 1963 by Kaye Starbird. Reprinted by permission of Paul R. Reynolds, Inc., 12 East 41st Street, New York, N. Y. 10017.

"Dos y Dos Son Cuatro" ("Two and Two are Four"), from *Play It in Spanish: Spanish Games and Folk Songs for Children.* Collected by Mariana Prieto. Music by Elizabeth Colwell Nielson. Copyright © 1973 by the John Day Company. Used by permission of Thomas Y. Crowell.

"The Duck in the Gun," from *The Duck in the Gun,* by Joy Cowley. Copyright © 1969 by Doubleday & Company, Inc. Reprinted by permission of Doubleday & Company, Inc., and the author.

"Giraffe," from *And the Frog Went "Blah!"* by Arnold Spilka. Copyright © 1972 by Arnold Spilka. Reprinted by permission of the author.

"The Goat in the Rug," adapted from *The Goat in the Rug,* by Charles L. Blood and Martin Link. Text copyright © 1976 by Charles L. Blood and Martin Link. Used by permission of Parents' Magazine Press.

Printed in the U.S.A.

ISBN: 0-395-31941-2

Contents

Spinners

MAGAZINE ONE

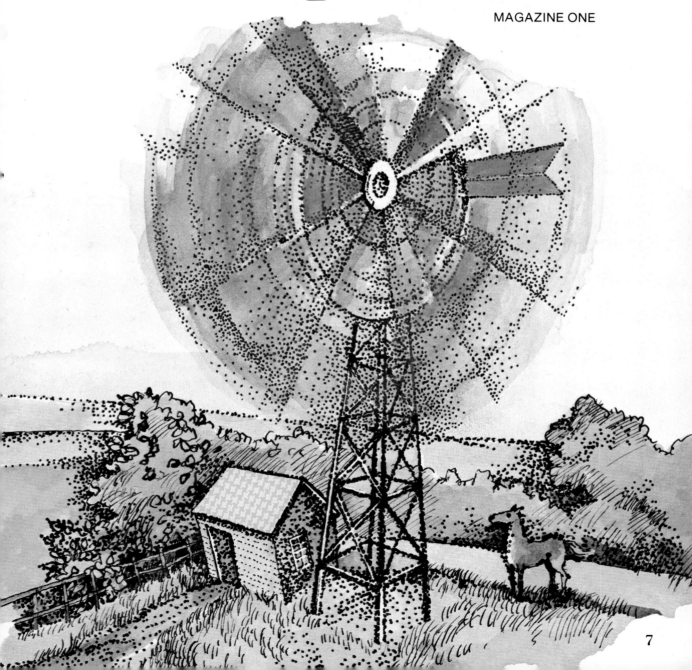

Contents

Keola's Hawaiian Donkey

by VIVIAN L. THOMPSON

Keola hummed a happy tune as he left his father's farm. It was a fine summer morning in Hawaii. The sky was blue. The grass was green. The air smelled of sweet blossoms.

Keola watched the people going to work in the coffee lands.

Keola stopped to watch a soft white cloud sail across the mountain top. The cloud looked like a white flower lei. But no one else was looking at it. Everyone else was hurrying by.

9

Keola saw Eugenio coming up the road, leading a small gray donkey. "Hi, Eugenio!" Keola called. "Isn't this a fine day? Look! The mountain has a lei of clouds around its neck!"

Eugenio said, "Bah! Who has time for clouds? I must take my new donkey to work on my coffee land."

The donkey, like Keola, was watching the clouds. But he pushed his nose against Keola's hand. Keola laughed and petted the donkey's soft gray nose. "What do you call him, Eugenio?"

Eugenio scowled. "I call him Paakiki because he is so stubborn. Come along, you stubborn donkey!"

Paakiki went along, but he looked back as if to say, "Keola, you come, too." So Keola went, too.

Soon they came to the coffee land. Keola watched the workers picking the coffee. When their baskets were full, they emptied them into big bags on the ground.

Keola helped Eugenio load two bags of coffee onto Paakiki's back. A light mist of rain began to fall. Keola lifted his face to the coolness of it.

"Let's go, Paakiki!" said Eugenio.

But Paakiki was enjoying the misty rain, too. He did not move.

"Come along, you stubborn donkey!" Eugenio cried. "We must take this coffee to the mill!"

Paakiki put his ears back and set his feet down hard.

Eugenio pulled!

Eugenio pushed!

Eugenio shouted!

But Paakiki would not move.

Eugenio tapped him with a coffee branch. Then Paakiki moved. He gave a sudden leap and started off.

Away went coffee bags!

Away went coffee pickers!

And away went Paakiki, lickety-split!

Keola cried, "I'll get him for you!" Into the road went Paakiki. Along came a line of cars.

Horns sounded!

Drivers shouted!

Keola caught the little donkey just in time. He led him back to Eugenio and said, "Paakiki will be a good donkey when he is older."

"Bah!" said Eugenio. "He will never be a good coffee land donkey. Maybe Takashi will buy him. Come along, you stubborn donkey!"

Paakiki went along, but he looked back as if to say, "Keola, you come, too." So Keola went, too.

Soon they came to a cane field. Eugenio called, "Takashi! You want to buy a donkey?"

Takashi said, "Sure! I need a donkey in my cane field." So Takashi bought Paakiki.

Keola watched the workers cutting sugar cane for seed. They cut the cane stalks into short pieces. Then they tied them in bundles. Keola helped Takashi load two bundles of cane stalks onto Paakiki's back.

The sun began to shine through the misty rain. Keola lifted his face to the warm sun.

"Let's go, Paakiki!" said Takashi.

But Paakiki was enjoying the warm sun, too. He did not move.

"Come along, you stubborn donkey!" Takashi cried. "We must take this cane to the planters."

Paakiki put back his ears and set his feet down hard.

Takashi pulled!

Takashi pushed!

Takashi shouted!

But Paakiki would not move.

Takashi tapped him with a piece of cane. Then Paakiki moved. He gave a sudden leap and started off.

Away went bundles of cane!

Away went field workers!

And away went Paakiki, lickety-split!

Keola cried, "I'll get him for you!" Across the field went Paakiki. Along came some cowhands, rounding up their cattle.

Horses leaped!

Cowhands yelled!

Keola caught the little donkey just in time. He led Paakiki back to Takashi and said, "He will be a good donkey when he is older."

"Bah!" said Takashi. "He will never be a good cane field donkey. Maybe Manuel will buy him. Come along, you stubborn donkey!"

Paakiki went along, but he looked back as if to say, "Keola, you come, too." So Keola went, too.

Soon they came to a taro patch. Takashi called, "Manuel! You want to buy a donkey?"

Manuel said, "Sure! I need a donkey in my taro patch." So Manuel bought Paakiki.

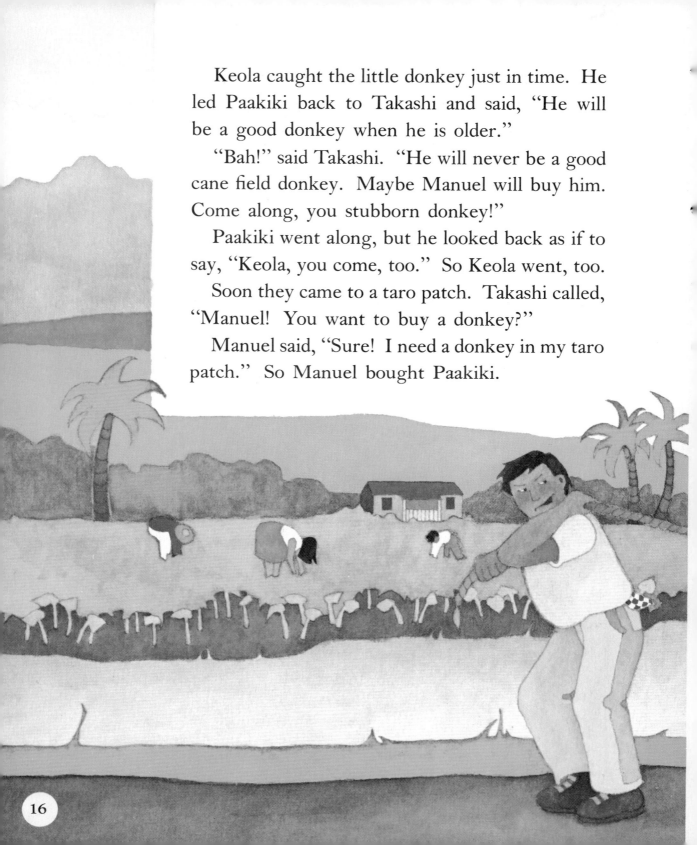

Keola watched as the workers pulled the taro plants from the water. The workers cut off the taro roots and threw them into big sacks. Keola helped Manuel load two sacks of taro onto Paakiki's back.

Keola looked ahead and saw a rainbow in the sky. He stopped to enjoy its glowing colors.

"Let's go, Paakiki!" said Manuel.

But Paakiki was enjoying the glowing colors of the rainbow, too. He did not move.

"Come along, you stubborn donkey!" cried Manuel. "We must take this taro to be made into poi."

Paakiki put back his ears and set his feet down hard.

Manuel pulled!

Manuel pushed!

Manuel shouted!

But Paakiki would not move.

Manuel tapped him with a taro plant. Then Paakiki moved. He gave a sudden leap and started off.

Away went sacks of taro!

Away went taro workers!

And away went Paakiki, lickety-split!

Keola cried, "I'll get him for you!" Into the road went Paakiki. Along came a great parade with a six-piece band.

Instruments flew!

Musicians shouted!

Keola caught the little donkey and led him back to Manuel. "He will be a good donkey when he is older," said Keola.

"Bah!" said Manuel. "He will never be a good taro patch donkey. What can I do with this donkey?"

"If you don't want him, would you let me have him?" Keola asked. "He could help me with work on our farm."

Manuel stared. "Keola, why would you want him? He would not work for Eugenio. He would not work for Takashi. He would not work for me. He is a stubborn one, this donkey!"

Keola laughed. He said, "He is not really stubborn. He is like me. I know there is work to be done, and work is important. But there are white clouds and misty rains and glowing rainbows. These are important, too. I take time for both, and so does this little donkey. He and I would be happy together!"

Manuel shook his head. He said, "Maybe you are right, Keola. If you want this donkey, then he is yours."

"Thanks, Manuel!" said Keola. "Come along, little donkey. It is time for us to get to work."

But Paakiki was watching the sunlight on the water. He did not move.

Keola laughed. He said, "You are right, little donkey. It is beautiful, and you are wise to take time to enjoy it. I think you should have a new name. Not Paakiki, the Stubborn One, but Akamai, the Wise One."

So Keola and Akamai, his wise Hawaiian donkey, took time to enjoy the beautiful sunlight together. And then they went home to work.

QUESTIONS

A. How were Keola and Paakiki alike?

B. How were Keola and Paakiki different from the others in the story?

C. Do you think Keola and Paakiki were wise to take time to enjoy rainbows and sunlight and misty rains? Why or why not?

D. Why do you think the clouds and glowing rainbows were important to Keola and Paakiki? What beautiful things are important to you?

I Meant To Do My Work Today

by RICHARD LE GALLIENNE

I meant to do my work today —
    But a brown bird sang in the apple-tree,
And a butterfly flitted across the field,
    And all the leaves were calling me.

And the wind went sighing over the land,
    Tossing the grasses to and fro,
And a rainbow held out its shining hand —
    So what could I do but laugh and go?

The Beautiful

HAWAIIAN

Above, above,
The birds flying.
Below, below,
The flowers on the earth.

In the mountains, the mountains,
The trees growing.
In the ocean, the ocean,
The fish of the sea.

Here ends my song,
The beautiful world.

The Unemployed Elephant

by LOUISE MOERI

One day Father Elephant said to Little Elephant, "Son, it's time you got a job."

Mother Elephant made Little Elephant a nice breakfast. Then she waved good-by to him as he set off to look for a job.

"Remember your manners. Be polite when you ask for a job!" she called.

That evening Little Elephant came home quite discouraged.

"Did you find a job?" asked Father Elephant.

"No," said Little Elephant. "I can't understand it. I was very polite. I took my hat off. And I said *please* and *thank you*. But I didn't get the job."

"Too bad," said Father Elephant. "What kind of job was it?"

"Bus driver."

Next day Little Elephant set out to look for a job again.

"Remember to dress nicely," said Mother Elephant. "Then you will make a very good impression when you ask for a job."

That evening Little Elephant came home quite discouraged.

"Did you get the job?" asked Father Elephant.

"No," said Little Elephant. "I tried so hard to make a good impression. I wore my new green hat and my new red tie with the yellow spots. And I carried my best umbrella. But I didn't get the job."

"Too bad," said Father Elephant. "What sort of job was it?"

"Selling the early-morning newspapers."

Next day Little Elephant set off again to find a job.

"Remember," said Mother Elephant. "Always get there early when you are looking for a job."

That night Little Elephant came home quite discouraged.

"Did you get the job?" asked Father Elephant.

"No," said Little Elephant. "I got there very early, too. In fact, the sun was hardly up. I got there earlier than anybody — even the boss. But I didn't get the job."

"Too bad," said Father Elephant. "What sort of job was it?"

"Guarding a bank at night."

Next day Little Elephant set off once more to find a job.

"Remember," said Mother Elephant. "You must know a lot about the job that you hope to get. You should find out beforehand as much as you can."

That evening Little Elephant came home quite discouraged.

"Did you get the job?" asked Father Elephant.

"No," said Little Elephant sadly. "I learned all I could about the job, too. I watched somebody do it. I even read three books about it at the library. But I didn't get the job."

"Too bad," said Father Elephant. "What kind of job was it?"

"Sorting eggs."

Everyone was quite discouraged. Would Little Elephant ever find a job? Mother and Father Elephant tried to be cheerful, but they were worried, too.

Then one day Little Elephant came racing home. "I got a job! I got a job!" he cried.

"Wonderful! Wonderful! What kind of job did you get?" cried Mother and Father Elephant.

"I did just what you told me to do," said Little Elephant. "I was polite. I dressed up nicely and made a good impression. I got there early. And, best of all, I knew a lot about the job."

"Wonderful!" Mother and Father Elephant cried. "What kind of job did you get?"

"Loading baggage at the bus station!" cried Little Elephant. "After all — who knows more about trunks than an elephant?"

QUESTIONS

A. What important things did Little Elephant learn about getting the right job?

B. Why would Little Elephant be better at loading baggage than at sorting eggs?

C. What other jobs can you think of that Little Elephant might do well? Why do you think so?

D. Have you ever thought about a job you might like to have someday? If so, why would you like to have that job?

Giraffe

by ARNOLD SPILKA

I'll tell you what it's like
  to be a giraffe.
First of all
  you're very careful
    about your neck.
So you never walk through
  revolving doors.
You don't eat ice cream
  because it never gets
    all the way down
    in time to taste like anything.
You don't have to climb over fences,
  you can easily reach
    over any of them.
With that very long, long neck
  you can do a lot of nice peeking.
But if it's very cold
  You must wear nine or ten scarves.
Does anybody want to be a giraffe?
Please raise your hand!

More Than One Meaning

Mark Climbed to the top of the high

Many words have more than one meaning. The word *bank* is one of them. In fact, the word *bank* has more than 20 meanings. You know some of the meanings. Others may be new to you. Suppose you came to the word *bank* in your reading. With so many meanings for the word, how could you decide which meaning to choose?

A good way to get the right meaning is to read and think about the other words in the sentence. Very often the other words will give you a clue to the meaning. What do the other words in the sentence below tell you about the word *bank?*

Jackie kept her money in a **bank.**

You can tell that a *bank* must be something you can keep money in. Most likely you already knew that meaning. But what about the word *bank* in the sentence below? What do the other words in the sentence tell you about the meaning of *bank?*

> Mark climbed to the top of the high **bank** of snow.

You have most likely decided that in this sentence, the word *bank* does not mean a place where you can keep money. That would not make sense with the other words in the sentence. The word *bank* must mean something else. The other words in the sentence tell you that this *bank* can be high. It can be made of snow, and you can climb to the top of it.

Below is another sentence using the word *bank*. This meaning of *bank* may be new to you. As you read, use the other words in the sentence to help you get the meaning.

Before she went to bed, Joan wanted to **bank** the fire with more wood so that it would keep burning all night.

You have most likely decided that in this sentence *bank* does not mean a pile of snow or a place to keep money. But what does it mean? The other words in the sentence tell you that *bank* must mean to add wood to a fire to keep it burning.

Using the other words in a sentence to help you get the right meaning for a word is called **using the context.**

GETTING THE RIGHT MEANING

As you read the sentences below, use the context to help you get the right meaning for each word in heavy black letters.

1. The British game of **cricket** is played with a bat and a ball.
2. We often go to the **spring** to get water.
3. Mark tried to **face** up to his problem.
4. The tall, woody tree **trunk** was covered with vines.
5. Karen's winter coat is very warm because it is filled with soft **down.**
6. The car became stuck in the sandy **shoulder** alongside the road.

Bus Ride   by NANCY JEWELL

Janie stared at the long silver bus that would take her to Grandpa's. It looked huge.

A man was putting suitcases and trunks into a big hole in the side of the bus.

Janie's mother was talking to a woman who was standing in line ahead of them.

"My name's Mrs. Rivers," said the woman, smiling at Janie. "We'll find seats on the bus together."

Papa gave Janie's ticket to the bus driver. Janie's stomach felt sort of funny — the way it did in an elevator.

"Remember," Mama said. "Grandpa will be there to meet you."

"Don't forget to wave to us from your seat," said Papa.

Mrs. Rivers found a pair of empty seats on the bus. "You take the window seat," she said. "I ride this old bus so often that I've seen just about everything there is to see. Besides, you've got to wave to your mama and papa."

Janie pressed her face against the cold, wet window glass. The bus began to move.

"Here I am!" Janie yelled, pounding on the glass until Mama and Papa saw her.

Janie stared out into the dark city streets. She wished Mama and Papa were sitting beside her.

In a few minutes, Mrs. Rivers handed Janie a big white handkerchief.

"You must be missing your mama and papa right now," Mrs. Rivers said, as she took an orange out of her pocketbook.

"Kind of," Janie said. But hearing Mrs. Rivers say that made the funny feeling in Janie's stomach go right away.

Mrs. Rivers cut a hole in the top of the orange and peeled it. She held out half of her orange to Janie.

"Here's your half, Janie," she said. "You'd be doing me a real favor to share this with me. I never can eat a whole orange anyway."

"Thanks," said Janie. She ate a cool, juicy piece of orange and looked out the window.

Now the bus was on a bridge going over a wide river. Far away, a long row of tall glass and silver buildings glowed with hundreds of tiny lights. Looking down, Janie could see green and red and yellow colors all mixed together and shining on the silver water.

"Now that's something to see," said Mrs. Rivers. "I never do get tired of that old city skyline at night."

Janie opened her paper bag of supper. She started to offer half of her chicken sandwich to Mrs. Rivers.

"You just break off a tiny bit for me," said Mrs. Rivers. "Your mama didn't mean for you to give your whole supper away."

After she finished eating, Mrs. Rivers said, "I think I'll take a little nap now. You be sure and wake me if you need anything or want somebody to talk to." Mrs. Rivers pushed a button on her chair arm to move the top part of her seat back. Janie pushed the button on her seat to see if it would move back, too. Then she pushed the button again and made the seat pop right back up.

It was very dark inside the bus now. Only a few overhead lights glowed inside. Janie could see a woman reading a magazine. The man next to her was eating chicken out of a box.

Over the low roar of the bus, Janie could hear lots of other sounds. A baby was crying. Someone was playing music at the front of the bus. It was fun sitting in the darkness, listening to the bus noises. And Janie liked the feeling of riding along in the bus. It ran so smooth and fast it almost seemed to be standing still.

"Wake up, Janie," said Mrs. Rivers.

"I wasn't asleep," Janie said, opening her eyes.

"You were out like a light for two whole hours," Mrs. Rivers said, smiling. "We're in the real country now. I didn't want you to miss seeing it."

Janie rubbed her eyes and looked out the window. Dark hills with round tops were all around them. The moon was so low it looked as if it were sitting right on top of a hill.

They went by a small house with a yellow light shining in one window. The house looked very small against the big hills and black sky.

"Do people get lonely here?" Janie asked.

"People get lonely anywhere, sometimes," Mrs. Rivers said. "Out here they get country lonely. That's different from city lonely."

"Are we almost there?" Janie asked.

Mrs. Rivers fished around inside her pocketbook. She took out a big alarm clock with yellow numbers that glowed in the dark. "If this old bus is on time," she said, "you'll be seeing your grandpa in ten minutes."

Now that they were so close, Janie didn't think she could wait another minute to see Grandpa. She combed her hair six times and tied and retied her shoelaces.

Finally the bus rolled to a stop.

"Looks like we have to say good-by to each other now, Janie," Mrs. Rivers said as she held Janie's hand. "But I've got a feeling we'll meet again on this old bus."

"Let's always sit together, Mrs. Rivers," Janie said. Part of her wanted to run to Grandpa. But another part of her wanted to stay on the bus with Mrs. Rivers.

"You hurry along now to your granddaddy," said Mrs. Rivers. "I'll wave from the bus."

As Janie left her seat, she could feel the cold air coming from the open bus door. The people ahead of her seemed to move as slow as turtles. Janie didn't think she'd ever get there. But finally Janie jumped off the bus right into Grandpa's arms.

Grandpa gave her a big hug. "I'll go and get your suitcase," he said.

Janie ran over to the bus. Mrs. Rivers opened the window and leaned out.

"Next time I ride this old bus," she called down, "I'll be looking for you to get on."

"Me too!" Janie shouted.

The bus began to move. Mrs. Rivers waved a white handkerchief out the window.

Janie waved back until the bus was only a silver spot in the darkness.

"That was Mrs. Rivers!" she told Grandpa. "We sat together the whole way from the city."

QUESTIONS

A. Do you think Mrs. Rivers knew how Janie felt at the beginning of the trip? What makes you think so?

B. What did Mrs. Rivers do to make Janie feel better?

C. What do you think Mrs. Rivers meant when she said that country lonely is different from city lonely?

D. By the end of the trip, how did Janie and Mrs. Rivers feel about each other?

The Bridge

by LILIAN MOORE

A bridge
by day
is steel and strong.
It carries
giant trucks that roll along
above the waters
of the bay.
A bridge is steel and might —
till night.

A bridge
at night
is spun of light
that someone tossed
across the bay
and someone caught
and pinned down tight —
till day.

VOCABULARY
How Slow Is Slow?

Big, little, fast, slow — these are words you say and hear all the time. Writers often use these words in a special way. Do you remember this sentence from the story "Bus Ride"?

> The people ahead of her seemed to move **as slow as turtles.**

In this sentence, the writer compares the people to turtles. Turtles are known for being slow. By comparing the people to turtles, the writer tries to give you a better idea of just how slowly the people seemed to be moving. They weren't just slow, they were *as slow as turtles.*

A sentence can be more interesting when a writer compares things like that. By comparing things, a writer can also help you to understand the sentence better. A writer may want you to get a picture in your mind of something you have never seen. So the writer compares it to something you *have* seen.

Suppose a writer wanted to tell people about a make-believe animal. Here are two ways the writer could do it:

> The **dinogoose** was big.
> The **dinogoose** was as big as an elephant.

Which sentence gives you a better picture of just how big the dinogoose was? You have never seen a dinogoose, but chances are you have seen an elephant. You can guess that a dinogoose must be very big.

There are many things that can be compared in this way. You may be surprised at how many things you compare every day as you talk. Do you ever say "as quick as a wink" or "as busy as a bee"? Listen to yourself and others, and you may hear many more things being compared.

The Mixed-Up Mystery Smell

by ELEANOR COERR

Kate raced across the yard to the clubhouse. She was carrying a box. A sign over the clubhouse door said:

DETECTIVES AT WORK.

GO AWAY.

Kate pushed the door open. "Hi! Look what I have," she yelled.

Her sister Marsha was talking to their friend Nobby. "Be quiet," Marsha said. "We're thinking of a mystery to solve."

"But I have a mystery," Kate said. "It's here in this box."

Marsha laughed.

"But I do," Kate said.

"Well, open it," Marsha told her.

Kate opened the box slowly. Marsha looked inside. "There's nothing here," she said.

Nobby looked with his magnifying glass. "I can't see anything," he said.

"There is something inside," Kate said. "It's a mystery smell." She stuck her nose inside the box and sniffed hard. Marsha and Nobby sniffed, too.

"I don't smell anything," Marsha said.

"I don't either," said Nobby.

"I've lost it!" Kate cried.

"That's OK," Marsha said. "You can *tell* us about it instead."

"You know that empty old house on Grizzly Hill?" Kate asked.

"You mean that spooky old place?" Nobby asked.

"That's it," Kate said. "But now you can see smoke coming out of it. And there's a funny smell all around it."

Marsha laughed. "Maybe a witch is in the house making a stew."

Kate shook her head. "It couldn't be that because it's not a bad smell. It's a kind of mixed-up smell."

"Whoever heard of a mixed-up smell?" Marsha asked.

"If you don't believe me," Kate said, "go and sniff for yourself."

"We don't have any other mysteries to solve today," said Nobby. "Kate, take us to the smell." Then Nobby put his detective notebook, a pencil, and a magnifying glass in his bag.

Kate led the way. They stopped in front of an old brown house. The wind blew dry leaves around the yard.

The house looked empty and spooky. Smoke curled up from the chimney. A strange smell was all around. Kate sniffed.

"Here it is!" she yelled. "Can you smell it?"

Nobby took a long sniff. "Hmmm," he said. "There *is* a smell. It makes me hungry." He wrote that down in his notebook.

Marsha sniffed. "You're right, Kate. You always did have the best nose in the family."

"Thanks!" said Kate.

"Well, we've got to solve this mystery," Marsha said. "Let's sniff and think."

They all sat down in front of the house. They thought of pancakes, apple pie, and brownies. They thought of fish, chicken, and steak. Nobby wrote them all in his notebook. But the mystery smell wasn't any of them.

Soon Kate got tired of sniffing and thinking. "My nose won't work anymore," she said. "Let's go around to the back — near the kitchen."

"Good thinking, Kate," Nobby said. "Maybe we'll find another clue."

They tiptoed around to the back of the house. The smell was stronger there. It came from an open window. But the window was too high to reach. Nobby found a box to stand on and put it under the window.

"Let me look first," Kate said. "It's *my* mystery smell." She climbed up and peeked into the kitchen.

"OOOO!" Kate said.

"What do you see?" Marsha whispered.

"Let me down!" Kate's eyes were huge. "I saw a ghost!" she told them.

"That's silly," Marsha said. "Let me look." She climbed onto the box.

"What do you see?" Nobby whispered.

Marsha jumped down. "A witch!" she cried. "With a tall white hat!"

"You're both crazy," Nobby said. "Let me up there." He took his turn on the box.

"WOW!" he said.

"What is it?" Marsha whispered.

"I see the back of a monster. It's pounding something on the kitchen table."

"Shhh!" said Marsha. "Be quiet and listen. It's talking."

A voice was saying, "I'll pound you and bump you and punch you hard." There were pounding, bumping, and thumping sounds. The voice went on. "Now you can rest and get fat. And then into the oven you go."

After that it was quiet.

Suddenly, CRASH! The window went down.

"Run!" Nobby yelled. He raced for the front of the house. Marsha was right behind him.

"Wait for me!" Kate called.

They didn't stop running until they were down the street and away from the house.

When they stopped running, Marsha said, "Something funny is going on in that house. If we are real detectives, we should go back and find out what it is."

"I guess you're right," Nobby said. They started back slowly.

The house looked even more spooky and empty. The kitchen window was still closed. Nobby looked at the wood under the window with his magnifying glass.

"I see a clue," he said. "The wood is wet."

"Of course it is," Marsha said. "It's beginning to rain!"

The sky grew darker. Big drops of rain came down.

"Listen," Marsha said. "I have a plan. And the rain will help."

"How?" Nobby asked.

"We'll go up to the front door and knock. We can say we were caught in the rain. There must be more clues inside the house."

"I'm not so sure," said Nobby. "I think we have enough clues already."

"Oh, come on," Marsha said. "We've got to see what lives there."

"You can go first this time, Marsha," Kate said.

Nobby and Kate followed Marsha up the steps. Marsha knocked on the door. There was no answer. There was just the sound of the rain and the mixed-up smell.

"Look at this!" Nobby said. "There's a note pinned to the door." The note said:

PLEASE COME INSIDE AND WAIT.

"How did it know we were coming?" he said. The hair on the back of his neck began to stand up.

Marsha pushed the door, and it squeaked open. They stood in the middle of a spooky room. The smell was very strong. Suddenly they heard a sound.

"Who moved?" Marsha whispered.

"I didn't," Nobby said. "Did you, Kate?"

"No," Kate said. "It wasn't me."

All at once, they made a dash for the door. Just then someone said loudly, "STOP! Don't run away."

At the same time, the lights went on.

The detectives looked around. An old woman stood near them. She didn't look like a witch or a ghost or a monster. She had a cheerful face, and on her head was a tall white hat.

"Who are you?" the woman asked.

"We are detectives," Marsha said. "I'm Marsha, and this is my sister Kate. Nobby is our friend."

"I'm Mrs. Birdie," the woman said. "What brings you detectives here?"

"We want to find out what makes the mixed-up smell," Marsha told her. "It's our mystery."

"It's *my* mystery," said Kate. "I found the smell first!"

"The note on the door said to come in," Nobby said. "So here we are."

Mrs. Birdie smiled and said, "That note was for someone else, but I'm glad you came. I just moved in last week, and I get lonesome." She smiled again. "Have you guessed what the smell is?"

"We tried," Nobby answered. "But we didn't have enough clues."

"Then follow me," Mrs. Birdie said. "I'll show you what makes the wonderful smell."

She led them through the house and into the kitchen. The warm kitchen was full of the smell. The three detectives stood in the doorway. They were almost afraid to look at the table.

Then they saw it.

There was a THING on the kitchen table.

It didn't look alive.

It wasn't even moving.

It was a big lump of something light brown.

Mrs. Birdie pointed to it.

"That's your mystery," she said.

"I know!" cried Marsha. "It's bread dough! We read about baking bread at school."

Kate was puzzled. "Our bread doesn't look like that," she said. "Or smell like that. Our bread comes in a bag from the store."

"Your bread *does* look like this before it's baked," Mrs. Birdie told Kate. "But I think my bread is much better because I make it with my own hands. That's why I hope people will come to buy it."

Mrs. Birdie gave them some of her fresh brown bread and butter. It tasted even better than it smelled.

"Then you aren't a witch!" Kate said.

Mrs. Birdie smiled. "No, I'm not a witch. But I do use magic. First you must be happy. If you are grouchy or sad, the bread won't come out right."

"Is that the magic?" Kate asked.

"Yes," said Mrs. Birdie. "That's part of it."

Then she showed them how to measure and mix. She showed them how to push and punch and pound the dough. And she told them about the bit of special magic — a plant called yeast.

"Yeast makes the dough come alive," she said.

"Then the lump of dough really is alive!" Kate said in surprise.

"Sort of," Mrs. Birdie said. "The yeast is mixed with water and a little sugar. Then the yeast begins to work. It makes gas in the dough. And then the dough grows bigger and bigger."

Nobby wrote it all down in his notebook. When the rain stopped, the detectives went home.

The next morning, they met in the clubhouse. The first thing they did was change the sign. Now it read:

DETECTIVES GONE FOR THE DAY. COME BACK LATER.

The second thing they did was to go to Kate and Marsha's house — to bake bread.

Soon they had a tasty, buttery, mixed-up smell of their own. And it wasn't a mystery any longer.

QUESTIONS

A. What do you think Kate, Nobby, and Marsha thought they would find in the old house?

B. Do you think Kate, Nobby, and Marsha were good detectives? Why or why not?

C. Do you think the children will go back to visit Mrs. Birdie? Why or why not?

Mrs. Birdie's Bread

by ELEANOR COERR

You can bake some of Mrs. Birdie's bread, too. First, BE HAPPY. If you are sad and grouchy, the bread won't come out right.

Make sure a grownup is nearby to help you. Wash your hands and clean a space on a table.

Here are the things you will need to bake Mrs. Birdie's bread. Make sure you have them ready before you begin.

Materials

small bowl	warm water
big bowl	cold water
teaspoon	dry yeast
tablespoon	brown sugar
measuring cup	milk
mixing spoon	salt
small pan	wheat germ
bread pan	vegetable oil
kitchen towel	whole wheat flour
potholders	unbleached flour

1. Get the small bowl. Put ½ cup of warm water in it. Add 2 packages of dry yeast. Then add 1 teaspoon of brown sugar. Stir everything with the mixing spoon and set the bowl aside.

2. Get the small pan. Slowly warm ½ cup of milk in the pan. Add 2 tablespoons of brown sugar. Put in 1 teaspoon of salt. Add 3 tablespoons of wheat germ and 2 tablespoons of vegetable oil. Warm and stir the mixture until the sugar is mixed in. Do not boil it.

3. Get the big bowl. Put the milk mixture from the pan into the big bowl. Add ½ cup of cold water. Add the yeast mixture from the small bowl. Stir everything with the mixing spoon.

4. Slowly stir 2 cups of whole wheat flour into the mixture in the big bowl. Slowly add and stir in 1 cup of unbleached flour.

5. Sprinkle a little flour on your hands. Mix the dough with your hands until it no longer feels sticky. You might have to add about ½ cup more of unbleached flour.

6. Now comes the fun — kneading.
    First sprinkle a little flour on the
    table and on your hands. Then
    take the dough out of the bowl
    and place it on the table.

    Push into the dough.
    Then fold it over.
    Push and fold again.

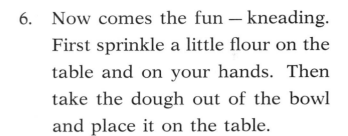

You will have to
do this many times.
Keep kneading until
the dough feels
rubbery and
smooth.

7. Clean out the big bowl and
    spread oil all over the inside of the bowl.
    Pat the dough into a nice ball and put it into
    the big bowl. Cover the bowl with a kitchen
    towel. Set it aside in a warm, dry place.

8. Wait for about 1 hour until the dough gets two times as big. Sprinkle a little flour on the table. Turn the ball of dough onto the table again. Punch the dough down hard. Then let it rest for about 5 minutes.

9. Get the bread pan. Spread oil over the inside of the pan. Pat the dough into a shape that will fit into the bread pan. Fit the dough into the pan. Cover it with a kitchen towel.

10. Set the bread pan in a warm, dry place for about ½ hour until the dough gets two times as big.

11. Turn the oven on to 400°. Wait 5 minutes and then put the bread pan into the oven.

12. Wait about 30 minutes. Then open the oven door and look at the bread. If the bread is brown, take it out of the oven. *Remember to use potholders!* Turn the bread out of the pan and let it cool.

Remember to turn off the oven and clean up the kitchen. Then you can enjoy some of Mrs. Birdie's bread. It will taste delicious.

QUESTIONS

A. What are some of the important steps in making Mrs. Birdie's bread?

B. Why is it important to read all the directions through first before you start to follow them?

C. Why do you think it is important to follow the steps in the right order?

Context:
A Clue to Word Meanings

When you are reading, you may come to a word that you have never seen before. You may have no idea what it means, but by using the context, you can often get the meaning.

You must read and think about the other words in the sentence. These other words can give you clues to the meaning of the word you don't know. Suppose you were reading a story, and you came to the word *mango*. What do the other words in this sentence tell you about the word *mango?*

My favorite fruit is a sweet, juicy **mango.**

From reading the other words in the sentence, you can tell that the word *mango* must mean some kind of fruit. The words *fruit, juicy,* and *sweet* are good clues to the meaning of the word *mango.*

Read the sentence below. What does the word *coyote* mean? What clues do you get from the other words in the sentence?

We thought we heard a **coyote** cry out in the night.

From the other words in the sentence, you can guess that *coyote* might mean some kind of animal. The other words in a sentence may be good clues, but they may not tell you enough about the word. You may need to read other sentences that come before or after the word.

Read the next two sentences. What new clues do you get to the meaning of the word *coyote?*

Earlier that day, I had seen a yellowish-brown animal running through the woods. It looked very much like a dog.

Now you know much more about the word *coyote.* You can usually get the meaning of a new word, such as *coyote,* by using the context — even if you are not sure how to say the word.

The context can be other words in the sentence or words in other sentences. The helpful parts of the context can come before or after the new word. Sometimes, the helpful parts come both before *and* after the word as in the sentence below:

> Before crossing the street, John waited for the **traffic** to go by, but the line of cars seemed to go on and on.

USING CONTEXT TO GET WORD MEANINGS

As you read the following sentences, use the context to help you get the meaning of each word in heavy black letters.

It started out to be a very **pleasant** day. It was warm and sunny. Laurie was sailing with Marsha, her older sister. Marsha was an **expert** sailor. She had won many sailing races in the family's **sloop.**

Before long, Laurie saw that the sky had become dark and **terrifying.** Laurie was frightened. She **imagined** the sloop tipping over in the wind. Marsha said, "Don't worry. We're not in trouble. Just stay **calm.** We'll be home before the storm."

A Bowl of Sun

by FRANCES WOSMEK

For a long time Megan had not even known that she was blind. Outside the house, Mike's strong hand had taught her how to move from place to place. Inside the house, she knew just where everything was. She could easily find her way from her own small bedroom to all the other rooms of the house.

Mike was Megan's father. He had a leather shop at the front of the house. He made fine leather belts, shoes, and bags to sell in his shop. The new leather was smooth and smelled better than almost anything.

Megan liked to help Mike as he worked. She made sandwiches for their lunch and swept up the bits of leather that fell to the floor.

Often on Sunday afternoons, Megan and Mike would walk down to the beach. Hand in hand, they would make a trail with their bare feet in the wet sand.

"Nobody lives a better life than we do," Mike always said. And Megan would smile up at him and agree.

Together they would build wonderful sand castles. Mike would hold Megan's hand in his, moving it over the sand. He would help her work with the wet sand until she learned to make the shapes he told her about.

One Sunday when they had finished a sand castle, Mike said, "The sun will soon be gone. It is time to go home. The sky is getting pink."

"Really pink?" Megan wanted to know.

"Pink as a rose," Mike answered.

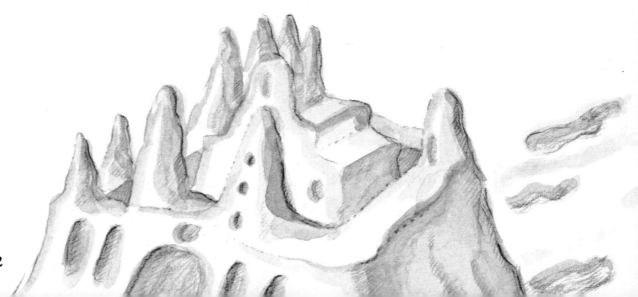

Megan smiled. She knew that pink was a happy color. The sound of Mike's voice told her that. She remembered the smell of a rose. "It must be a very happy sky," she thought. She put her hand in Mike's and they started for home.

Suddenly, Megan's happy, familiar world turned upside down. She heard Mike's voice trying its best to make her understand what was happening.

"We are going to move," he told her.

"Move?" said Megan.

Megan had never thought of moving. She knew that there were other people and places, but they had never seemed quite real to her before.

"We are moving to Boston," Mike went on. "You will go to school. You know it cannot always be just the two of us. You must have a chance to learn to live your life in your own way."

For a few minutes, no one said anything at all.

"You will learn to read," Mike said. "Reading is a way of knowing things."

Megan did not reply. She could think of nothing that she did not already know.

"In the school where you will go," Mike went on, "the children learn to read with their hands. People whose eyes cannot see can have their hands trained to take the place of the eyes. The school you will go to is near Boston."

Mike said he would work in a leather shop in Boston. The new shop, he told Megan, would be a lot bigger than the one he had now. He and Megan would live in an apartment house near the new shop. A lot of people Mike knew lived there, too. "That way," Mike explained, "you will not be alone when I work late at the shop."

Megan's new world was strange to her. There were sounds of traffic, horns, and strange voices that never stopped. It was a world of unfamiliar places and things.

Megan felt alone and helpless. She waited to be taken from this place to that, from her new home to her new school, and back again. She didn't try to do anything by herself.

Mike was worried and upset. "She has never been so helpless," he told his friend Rose. Rose lived in another apartment in the same building. She made clay pots on a wheel.

"It will take time," Rose told him. "It is a change that is not easy for her. She will learn to like us. You will see."

"Back home," Mike said sadly, "I would almost forget that she couldn't see. She did everything by herself. I thought she needed a school and other people. Maybe I was wrong."

"Don't worry," said Rose. "It will work out."

But things did not seem to be working out at all. Every day after school, Megan sat alone by the open window remembering the smell of the sea. When she heard the loud, rattling sounds of the busy city, she remembered the gentle sound of the waves washing up onto the sand.

Sometimes Rose took Megan to Mike's shop. The smell of the leather was the same. But now Mike did not need Megan's help. Someone else cleaned up the shop and swept up the bits of leather.

Mike talked to Megan's teachers at school. "Megan is no trouble," they told him. "But she will not try to do anything by herself. You must do your best to help."

One morning, Mike said to Megan, "Have Rose bring you down to the shop after school. We will go for a walk in the park when I am through working. And we can go for a boat ride on the pond. I will show you what a nice place the city really is."

Megan smiled. "I'd like that very much," she said.

Megan was really excited. She and Mike would have fun together — just the two of them! It would be like old times.

Megan could think of nothing else all day but Mike and the park. The bus ride home from school had never seemed so slow.

Finally Megan was at Rose's door. She knocked softly. Then she stepped back, waiting for the door to open. But nothing happened. She knocked again. There was no answer.

Suddenly Megan felt very much alone. What could she do? Mike would be waiting. He would be worried if she did not come.

Then, in a flash, Megan knew what she must do. She must go to Mike's shop alone. The shop was not far away. She had gone there many times with Rose. She was quite sure that she remembered the way. Mike would be so pleased that she had found the way by herself.

Megan knew the way down the stairs and out the front door. She went down the outside steps, counting each one.

Megan could hear the traffic rolling past the apartment house. She turned in the direction she remembered. She walked carefully and listened for every sound. People raced by. Everyone seemed in a very great hurry. Then Megan was surprised by the sudden bark of a dog.

Megan began to worry. Was this the right way to Mike's shop? Maybe she should turn back. But then she thought of Mike. He would be so pleased to think she had found the shop by herself. She walked on slowly and carefully.

Soon Megan came to a corner. She slowly stepped into the street.

"Look out for the traffic, little girl!" she could hear a woman's voice say. "Can't you see that the light is red?"

Megan made no reply. Now she was really afraid. The woman looked down at her.

"No, of course you can't see the light," the woman added kindly. "Where do you live?"

"I know where she lives," another voice said. It was a voice that Megan knew. It was Rose.

"I'm awfully sorry, Megan," Rose said. "I was so busy working that I didn't hear you knock. When I noticed how late it was, I came looking for you."

"Can we still go to the shop?" Megan asked.

"I really am sorry," Rose said. "I'm afraid it's too late for that today." Rose took Megan's hand and they started for home.

When they were back in Rose's quiet apartment, Rose called Mike. Mike said that he would take Megan to the park tomorrow instead.

"Come, Megan," said Rose. "I will show you my potter's wheel. If you like, I will teach you how to make a bowl of clay."

Rose took Megan's hands in hers and began to guide them over the potter's wheel. She explained how the wheel helped her to form the clay pots and bowls.

Rose threw a piece of wet clay onto the middle of the wheel. She started the wheel turning. Then she took Megan's hands and slowly guided them to shape the clay into a bowl.

Megan could feel the cool, wet clay turn in her hands. As she worked with the clay, she forgot about how unhappy she had been in the city. But she remembered the sea. She remembered the sand castles that she and Mike had made. She thought of the sun going down in the pink sky.

Then, for a long time, she thought of nothing else but Rose's words and hands, as they guided her own.

By suppertime Rose was quite pleased. "I never knew anyone who learned so fast!" she said to Megan.

"I'd like to make a bowl for Mike," Megan said. "But I want it to be a surprise."

Rose smiled. "I will teach you how to make a bowl all by yourself. I think it may be the nicest surprise that Mike ever had."

Megan's world suddenly seemed to be filled with sunshine. Everything began to seem wonderful and exciting.

"I can't believe it," said Mike, shaking his head. "Why should things suddenly change for her?"

Rose just smiled and said nothing. She kept their secret.

Megan's teachers were pleased. "Megan seems so much happier," they all agreed. "She is learning to read and to do so many more things for herself."

Every afternoon after school, Megan sat at Rose's wheel and practiced. The cool clay slipped through her hands. Little by little, she learned to shape it.

Finally Megan and Rose agreed that one of the bowls was better than all the others.

"I will bake it in my clay oven," Rose explained. "The heat will make the clay hard. The bowl can have a color, too, if you like."

It took Megan no time at all to decide on a color. "The bowl must be pink," she said. "It must be pink as the sky when the sun goes down."

One day when Mike came home from the shop, Megan was all excited. "I have a surprise for you, Mike!" she cried. "It's a surprise that Rose and I have been working on for a long time. Come on! Let's go down to her apartment and you can see it."

When Megan placed the bowl in Mike's hands, she waited excitedly to hear what he would say.

For what seemed like a very long time, Mike said nothing at all. Then he turned to Rose. "Did Megan really make this all by herself?" he asked. Megan could hear the surprise in his voice.

"Yes," Rose answered. "Megan could be a very good potter, Mike. She hardly needs to be taught."

Mike put the bowl down carefully. He gave Megan a big hug. "Someday you will have your own potter's wheel," he said. "Then, when you are through with school, maybe we can be partners in a shop beside the sea."

"Oh, I'd like that!" said Megan. "And maybe Rose can be a partner, too."

"Maybe," Mike agreed. "Maybe she could be a partner at that!"

Megan smiled happily. The room felt as warm as a friendly hand.

QUESTIONS

A. Why did moving to a new place make Megan unhappy and helpless?

B. How did Rose teach Megan to make a bowl of clay?

C. How was building sand castles like making a clay bowl?

D. How did Megan learn about the places around her?

E. Why do you think learning to make a clay bowl made Megan feel happy?

Hands

by BOBBI KATZ

Clapping
slapping
finger-snapping
folding
holding
modeling
molding
writing
fighting
stroking
poking
itching
stitching
shaking
taking
squeezing
teasing
pleasing
HANDS!

Old Ben Bailey Meets His Match

by MAY JUSTUS

Many years ago, Big Les and his son Lester lived in No-End Hollow and raised dogs for a living. Their dogs were the finest foxhounds in all that part of Tennessee. People came from North Carolina, Georgia, and Alabama to buy foxhounds from them.

Now Lester had a pet hound dog that was not for sale to anybody. Funny Face was his name — Funny for short. Lester could have sold Funny for as much as sixty dollars. And that was a mighty lot of money at that time. But Lester loved Funny too much to sell him to anybody.

Funny followed Lester everywhere he went. That fall, when school started, the teacher made a rule that said all dogs had to be left at home. It would break Funny's heart to be left behind. Lester didn't want to leave him, but there was nothing else to do.

As Lester was on his way to school one morning, he heard a familiar bark. Funny was racing after him. Lester felt so sorry for the dog that he hadn't the heart to scold him. He petted him for a minute or two. Then he said, "I'll have to take you home again, even if it makes me late to school."

As they were going up the hollow, they had to pass right by Old Ben Bailey's place. Old Ben was standing by his front fence. When he saw Lester and Funny, he understood what had happened.

"Too bad about your dog running away," he said. "Now you'll be late to school, and you'll likely get in trouble for that. But I have a fine idea, Lester. Leave your dog here with me and pick him up on your way home this afternoon."

Lester thought for a minute. He knew Old Ben Bailey wasn't to be trusted. It was said that Old Ben would steal chickens and turkeys. But worst of all, he was thought to be a dog thief.

Lester had heard these stories about Old Ben. But he didn't think Funny would be in any trouble. Old Ben wouldn't be likely to steal the dog right in the middle of the day.

"Mighty thankful to you for the favor," Lester said to Old Ben Bailey. With a final pat for Funny, he left him and hurried on to school. He was barely in time.

Lester tried hard to do his lessons. But he kept thinking about leaving Funny with Old Ben. Something told him he shouldn't have done that.

This thought was such a worriment to him that he missed three words in his spelling lesson. Mr. Rector, the teacher, kept him after school to learn them.

When he got out at last, Lester raced up the trail in such a hip-and-hurry that he bumped his toe. Lester was limping badly by the time he reached Old Ben's house.

Old Ben was leaning on the fence. But there was no sign of Funny.

"Where — where . . ." Lester stopped.

"Son, I have bad news for you," said Old Ben Bailey, speaking in a sad voice. "Your dog is gone away, gone for good. I'm sorry to tell you, but this is how it happened."

"After you left," he went on, "Funny just rolled over and played dead like a possum. I tried to cheer him up. I talked to him. I gave him a piece of bread. No use. He kept right on playing dead. And then, right down from out of the sky sailed a big turkey buzzard. It flew away with him clean over the mountain top! Too bad, but that's what happened."

And Old Ben shook his head sadly.

Now Lester did not believe a word of this crazy story. He knew Old Ben had hidden Funny. Old Ben would sell Funny far away from there. Lester knew Old Ben was putting on a sad face just to fool him, and that he was laughing on the other side of his mouth.

Just then a mule that was standing in the yard threw back its head and went "Hee haw!" Lester felt as if the mule were laughing at him, too, just like Old Ben. It was all Lester could do to keep from shouting out.

Then an idea popped into Lester's head.

He limped around a step or two and looked at his bumped toe.

"Mr. Ben Bailey," he said. "My toe hurts mighty bad. Would you let me ride your mule on home?"

"I guess I could do you that favor," said Old Ben. "I'll need him early in the morning. But you can bring him back on your way to school."

Lester remembered that the next day was Saturday. But he didn't say anything about it because of the plan that had popped into his head. He jumped on the mule in a hip-and-hurry. Then he remembered his manners.

"Mighty thankful for the favor," he called to Old Ben as he headed up the trail for home.

The next morning Big Les and Lester were outside digging sweet potatoes. About ten o'clock, along came Old Ben Bailey. He was mad as a hornet.

"Where's my mule, Lester?" he yelled. "I told you to bring him back this morning, bright and early, on your way to school."

"But it's Saturday," Lester said. "I don't go to school on Saturday. I stay home and help dig sweet potatoes."

"Never mind making excuses like that," Old Ben Bailey said. "Where is my mule? That's all I want to know. And I want to find out in a hurry!"

Old Ben Bailey's face was as red as a bowl of pickled beets. He shook his finger right in Lester's face.

Lester answered sadly, "Mr. Ben Bailey, I'm sorry to tell you what happened to your mule. Why, as soon as I got home yesterday, I turned him out in the field. He ate grass for a while, and then he stretched out to rest. That's when the turkey buzzards got him. A whole flock flew away with him."

Old Ben Bailey jumped up and down. "That's a lie-tale you're telling!" he shouted. "No flock of turkey buzzards could fly away with a mule."

Big Les stepped up then and laughed a laugh that ran up and down the hollow.

"The turkey buzzards around here are mighty strong," Big Les said. "If one buzzard can carry off a full-grown foxhound, a whole flock of buzzards wouldn't have any trouble flying off with a mule!"

Big Les laughed again, and Lester laughed with him.

Old Ben Bailey turned all of a sudden and headed off down the trail. For once he felt outfoxed, and he couldn't think of another word to say.

While they were eating supper that night, Lester and his pappy heard a familiar bark outside the back door.

When they let Funny in, as you may believe, there was a great hip-and-hurrah. No telling which was happiest, the boy or his dog!

Old Ben Bailey's mule woke him up with a loud "hee-haw" next morning. Old Ben looked out his door to see the mule eating grass in the yard.

This might have been the end of the tale, but of course it wasn't. The news went up and down No-End Hollow and traveled over Near-Side and Far.

"Lester beat Old Ben at his own game," people said.

Old Ben met the tale wherever he went, going or coming. And it made him so mad that he moved to Far-Side.

QUESTIONS

A. Who was Old Ben Bailey's "match"? How did Old Ben Bailey "meet his match"?

B. Why was Old Ben so angry at Lester?

C. How did Old Ben know that Lester was fooling him?

D. People said that Lester had beaten Old Ben at his own game. What did this mean?

The Way It Was

This is the way many schools looked 100 years ago. Schools look very different today.

What things are different?

What things are the same?

Books to Enjoy

The Wonderful Box by Mildred Ames

When three children find a mysterious box, they have to wait and wonder about it for thirty days.

The Contest at Cowlick by Richard Kennedy

Young Wally saves the town by tricking a bank robber and his gang.

Tracy by Nancy Mack

How a girl with cerebral palsy gets along with other children makes an interesting story.

Speedboat by James Marshall

Jasper and his best friend have many adventures in a speedboat and at home.

How to Make Possum's Honey Bread by Carla Stevens

In this funny story, Possum tries to teach his friends how to make tasty bread.

Spinners

MAGAZINE TWO

Contents

Yagua Days

by CRUZ MARTEL

It was raining on the Lower East Side of New York City. From the doorway of his family's *bodega*, Adan Riera watched the rain pounding on the sidewalk.

School had ended for the summer two days ago, and for two days it had rained. Adan wanted to play in East River Park. But with so much rain, there wasn't much to do but watch cars splash by.

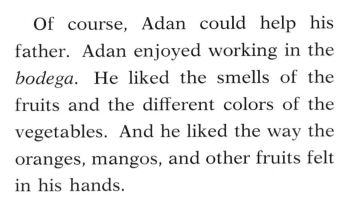

Of course, Adan could help his father. Adan enjoyed working in the *bodega*. He liked the smells of the fruits and the different colors of the vegetables. And he liked the way the oranges, mangos, and other fruits felt in his hands.

But today he would rather be in the park. He watched a car splash by. The rain began to fall even harder.

Jorge came into the *bodega*, carrying his mail bag. He shook the water off his hat and smiled at Adan. *"Hola,* Adan! Why the long face?"

"Rainy days are terrible days," answered Adan.

"No — they're wonderful days. They're *yagua* days!" Jorge said.

"Oh, Jorge!" said Adan. "Yesterday you told me that the vegetables and fruits in the *bodega* are grown in trucks! What is a *yagua* day?"

"This rainy day is a *yagua* day," Jorge replied. "And Puerto Rican vegetables and fruits are grown in trucks. Why, I have a truck myself. Every day I water it!"

Adan's mother and father came in from the back of the *bodega*.

"*Hola*, Jorge. You look wet," said Mother.

"I feel wetter," said Jorge. "But it is a wonderful feeling. It's a *yagua*-day feeling!"

Adan's mother and father liked Jorge. They had all grown up together in Puerto Rico.

"So you've been telling Adan about *yagua* days?" asked Adan's father.

"*Sí*, I have. Look. Here's a letter for you from our hometown, where we all had some of the best *yagua* days."

Adan's father read the letter. "Good news!" he said. "My brother Ulise wants us to visit him on his plantation for two weeks."

"You haven't been to Puerto Rico in years," said Jorge.

"Adan's never been there," replied his mother. "We could ask my brother to take care of the *bodega*. Adan will meet his family in the mountains at last."

Jorge smiled. "Maybe you'll even have a few *yagua* days. Have fun!"

Welcome to Puerto Rico

Uncle Ulise met Adan and his mother and father at the airport. "Welcome to Puerto Rico, Adan."

Uncle Ulise had tiny blue eyes in a round red face, and big strong arms. But Adan, excited after his first plane ride, hugged Uncle Ulise even harder than Uncle Ulise hugged him.

"Come, we'll drive to the plantation." Uncle Ulise smiled at Adan's father. "I'm sorry you didn't get here yesterday," he said. "Yesterday was a wonderful *yagua* day."

"You know about *yagua* days, too, Uncle Ulise?" asked Adan.

"They're my favorite days," said Uncle Ulise.

"But wouldn't today be a good *yagua* day?" asked Adan.

"Not at all," replied his uncle. "The sun's out!"

They rode up into the mountains with Uncle Ulise in his truck.

"Look!" said Uncle Ulise. "Your mother and father and Jorge and I played in that river when we were children."

At the top of a hill, they saw a group of bright houses. Adan saw a crowd of people standing outside.

"This is your family, Adan," said Uncle Ulise.

Everyone crowded around Uncle Ulise's truck. Old people and young people. Brown-haired, black-haired, and light-haired people. Dark-skinned and light-skinned people. Adan had not known there were so many people in his family.

Aunt Carmen gave Adan a big hug. She made Adan feel very much at home.

The whole family sat under wide trees and ate tasty Puerto Rican food.

Adan talked and sang until his voice turned to a squeak. He ate until his stomach almost popped his buttons.

And before the sun had even gone down behind the mountains, Adan was asleep under a big net.

In the morning, Uncle Ulise called out, "Adan, we ate all the food in the house. Let's get more."

"From a *bodega?*" asked Adan.

"No, from my plantation on the mountain," Uncle Ulise explained.

"Do you drive a tractor on the mountain?" asked Adan.

Aunt Carmen smiled. "We don't need tractors on our plantation," she said.

"I don't understand," said Adan.

"You will," she promised.

Adan and his mother and father, Aunt Carmen, and Uncle Ulise walked up the mountain beside a splashy stream. Near the top, they walked through groves of fruit trees.

"Long ago your grandfather planted these trees," Adan's mother said. "Now Aunt Carmen and Uncle Ulise pick what they need for themselves. Some of the fruit they give away or sell in town."

"Let's get to work!" said Aunt Carmen.

Adan sat on his father's shoulders and picked oranges. He pulled down the sweet golden mangos. He watched Uncle Ulise chop down breadfruit, and he helped Aunt Carmen dig the potato-like *ñames* from the ground.

"How do we get all the food down the mountain?" Adan asked.

"Watch," said Aunt Carmen. She gave a loud whistle.

Adan saw something moving in the trees. It was a beautiful white horse. Uncle Ulise gave the horse a *guanábana*. The horse quickly ate the sweet fruit.

"The horse will help us carry all the fruit and vegetables we've picked," Adan's mother said.

Back at the house, Adan gave the horse another *guanábana.*

"The horse will go back up to the plantation now," his father said. "He has all he wants to eat up there."

Uncle Ulise sat down and rubbed his knee.

"What's wrong?" asked Adan's mother. "Is your knee hurting you?"

"Yes. It always hurts just before rain comes."

Adan looked at the cloudless sky. "But it's not going to rain."

"Yes, it is! My knee never lies. It will rain tonight. Maybe tomorrow. But when it does, it will be a *yagua* day!"

In the morning when Adan woke up, he could hear it raining. He could hear the little tree frogs, called *coquís,* beeping like tiny car horns.

Adan jumped out of the bed. His mother and father, Uncle Ulise, and Aunt Carmen were in their bathing suits.

"Put on your bathing suit, Adan," his father said. "It's a wonderful *yagua* day!"

Adan could hear shouts and swishing noises coming from the forest. He raced toward the sounds. He saw boys and girls sliding down a runway of grass and then disappearing over a rock ledge.

Uncle Ulise picked up something from the grass. "This is a *yagua*, Adan," he said. "It fell from this palm tree."

"And this is what we do with it," said Adan's father. He ran and then flopped onto the *yagua*. He slid down the grass, sailed up into the air, and disappeared over the ledge. His mother found another *yagua* and did the same.

"*Papi! Mami!*" cried Adan.

Uncle Ulise laughed. "Don't worry, Adan. They won't hurt themselves. The river is down there. It forms a pool under the ledge. The rain makes the grass slippery so you can slide right into the water. That's what makes it a *yagua* day! Come and slide with us."

That day Adan found out what fun a *yagua* day is!

Home Again

Two weeks later Adan was back in New York.

"*Hola*, Adan! Welcome home!" called Jorge.

Adan smiled at Jorge. "You look sad, my friend," Adan said.

"Too much mail! Too much sun!" said Jorge.

"What you need is a *yagua* day," said Adan.

"So you know what a *yagua* day is?" asked Jorge.

"I had six *yagua* days in Puerto Rico," Adan told him.

"You went over the ledge?" asked Jorge.

"Of course," said Adan.

"Into the river?" asked Jorge.

Adan laughed. "*Sí! Sí!* Into the river. Sliding on *yaguas!*"

"Two-wheeled or four-wheeled *yaguas?*" asked Jorge.

Adan laughed again. "*Yaguas* don't have wheels. They come from palm trees."

"I thought they came from trucks like mine."

"Nothing grows in trucks, Jorge. These mangos and oranges come from trees," explained Adan. "The peas come from bushes. And the *ñames* come from under the ground. My friend, wake up! You know that!"

Jorge laughed. "Come, country boy! Let's talk with your father and mother. I want to hear all about your visit to Puerto Rico!"

QUESTIONS

A. Why do you think Adan's mother and father were excited about their trip to Puerto Rico?

B. What were some of the things Adan learned when he was in Puerto Rico?

C. How was life on Uncle Ulise's plantation different from life in New York City?

D. What things could Adan do in New York City that would be as much fun as sliding on *yaguas?*

Puerto Rico

Hola! Welcome to Puerto Rico — one of the most beautiful islands in the Caribbean Sea.

Puerto Rico is a very special place. It has long, white sandy beaches lined with tall, green palm trees.

The middle of the island has high mountains. They are partly covered with a blanket of thick green bushes, trees, and brightly colored flowers.

The weather in Puerto Rico is always warm. People can go swimming all year long. In the mountains, there are often heavy rainfalls, but it rains for just a short time. Soon it is sunny again.

Many different fruits grow well in such warm weather. Bananas, mangos, and pineapples are just some of the delicious fruits that are grown by farmers in the countryside, called *el campo*.

117

Puerto Rico has small villages and towns and some very large cities. The largest city is San Juan. It has many tall office buildings and hotels.

Many Puerto Ricans work in offices, stores, and other businesses. The people of Puerto Rico speak and write in Spanish.

Someday you may be able to visit Puerto Rico. Then you can discover for yourself that it is a very special place.

QUESTIONS

A. What were some of the different places in Puerto Rico that you read about?

B. How is the Puerto Rican countryside different from the city of San Juan?

C. What part of Puerto Rico would you like to visit? Why?

Dos y Dos Son Cuatro

(Two and Two Are Four)

Dos y dos son cuatro,
Cuatro y dos son seis,
Seis y dos son ocho,
Y ocho dieciseis.

Two and two are four,
Four and two are six,
Six and two are eight,
And eight are sixteen.

YUCATAN

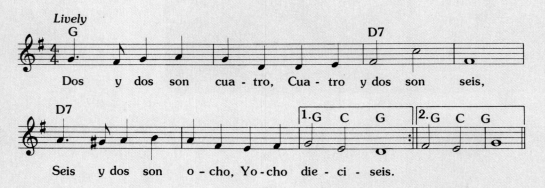

Dos y dos son cua-tro, Cua-tro y dos son seis,

Seis y dos son o-cho, Yo-cho die-ci-seis.

Mary of Mile 18

by ANN BLADES

It had been a cold winter in northern British Columbia. At the farm where Mary lived, snow had covered the ground since early November and would not melt until May.

One clear night in March, the northern lights flashed across the sky. Mary went to the window to watch. She liked to think that if she saw the northern lights, the next day would bring something special.

Mary of Mile 18 © 1971, Ann Blades. Published by Tundra Books Inc.
Reprinted from *Mary of Mile 18* © 1971 by Ann Blades, published by Tundra Books of Montreal. This text has been adapted and simplified from the original using a vocabulary familiar to younger readers.

The next morning, Mary woke up feeling a little excited. At first she couldn't think why. One winter day was so much like the next. And then she remembered the northern lights. Maybe today would bring something special.

Mary put on her warm clothes and went out to the hen house. She fed the chickens and then started back to the house. As she looked at the house, Mary remembered another special day — the day her father finished building the house. He had been so proud.

Now Mary saw her father near the barn, fixing the tractor. Every winter day that it wasn't snowing, Father liked to clear a little more land. He used the tractor to push the trees down and into piles. In the summer, the family would dig up tree roots so that more land could be planted.

After breakfast, there was still a little time before Father had to drive the older children to school. Father was playing with little Eva, and Jake and Isaac were reading. Mary liked this time of day. She often played a game with her sister Sarah, but today Mary couldn't keep her mind on the game. What special thing could happen today? Would it happen at school? She couldn't wait to get there and find out.

Father went out first and started the truck. When he had let it run for a while, he blew the horn. Mary, Sarah, Jake, and Isaac came out and crowded into the truck. It was a tight fit, but it was also nice and warm.

In school, Mrs. Burns had turned the oil heater on full. But the room was still so cold that the children sitting beside the windows kept their coats on and moved closer to the heater. At noontime, Sarah watched the class while Mrs. Burns had her lunch. At three o'clock, Mary helped the smaller children with their coats and boots.

Mary sighed as she pulled on her own boots. School was over for the day, and still nothing special had happened.

In the truck on the way home, Father listened to the children talk about school but didn't talk himself. It had started to snow, and he was watching the road very carefully. The snow was blowing, and it was hard to see.

Just as they came near their farm, another truck suddenly loomed out of the blowing snow. Father quickly steered the truck to the right to keep from crashing into the other truck. The back wheels of his truck slid off the road.

Mary watched as her father put chains on the back tires. "I hope *that's* not the special thing," she thought.

Then, farther up the road, Mary saw something in the snow. "Look, a puppy!" she cried. She ran to the puppy and held her hand out toward it. The puppy licked her hand. She picked the puppy up and carried it back to the truck.

"Please, Father, can I keep him?" she asked.

Father shook his head. "You know the rules, Mary. We don't have enough money to have an animal just as a pet. Our animals must work for us or give us food."

"But a dog can help—"

Father stopped her. "This is a different kind of dog, Mary. He's part wolf, and wolf-pups are useless to us. Take him into the woods and leave him."

While Father finished getting the truck back on the road, the other children walked the rest of the way home to do their chores. Sadly Mary went off with the puppy. He snuggled in her arms as she carried him into the woods. How she wished she could keep him! "I would call you Wolf," she said.

It had stopped snowing, but the path in the woods was covered over and could not be seen. If Mary went too far from the road, she might not be able to find her way back. She put the puppy down to see what would happen. He ran around and sniffed at the trees. Mary turned and walked away. The puppy did not follow.

"That was something special, all right," thought Mary as she walked home. "But it didn't last for long."

Near the house, Mary passed Isaac riding their horse, Mouse. When they were smaller, Isaac and Jake rode Mouse to school. But now Mouse had to wait until Isaac got home to go for a run.

The house smelled of fresh-baked bread as Mary came in.

"Where have you been, Mary?" asked her mother. "Sarah is waiting for you. I'm almost out of water."

Silently Mary picked up the two empty buckets near the door and went out. Then she and Sarah filled the buckets with snow. The two girls carried the snow, a bucket at a time, into the house and emptied it into a big barrel. From the barrel would come all the water for drinking, cooking, and washing.

Mary and Sarah emptied their buckets into the barrel many times before it was full. Each time Mary went back out, she looked toward the woods. Father came out of the barn, and Isaac came back with Mouse. The puppy was nowhere to be seen.

Just before suppertime, Mary was sitting at the table. But she was only staring at the book in front of her. It was going to be another very cold night, and she was thinking about the puppy.

Suddenly there was a sound outside the door. Father went to the door and opened it.

"It's little Wolf!" cried Mary. She hurried to take the puppy in her arms.

Father was angry. "Mary, don't encourage that dog to stay around! Get your coat on and get him out of here so that he doesn't come back!"

This time Mary walked along the road to the nearest farm almost two miles away. "Maybe Mrs. Bergen will let her children keep you. Then I could see you sometimes," she said. She put Wolf down near the Bergens' door.

Mary ran home quickly in the cold night. The cold bit her toes and fingertips, and the air burned her face.

The family was at the supper table when she got back. Her mother said, "We're having your favorite supper tonight, Mary. Moose steak."

"I don't want to eat, Mother," said Mary.

Mother started to say something, but Father stopped her. "Let the girl go to bed without eating if she wants to," he said. His voice was still angry. "She should not have asked to keep the animal. She knows the rules."

Mary went to bed, but she could not go to sleep. "Why should Father be so angry?" she wondered. Then she remembered that last fall Jake and Isaac begged their father for a second horse. He told them no and got angry then, too. Her mother explained, "Your father gives you everything he can. When you ask for more, it hurts him to refuse. That is why he gets angry."

Mary thought about this for a long time. Then she finally fell asleep.

Late that night, a coyote came out of the woods. It sniffed at all the buildings and stopped at the hen house. Silently the coyote pawed at the rope that held the door shut. The rope came untied. The coyote pushed the door open and went into the hen house to get at the chickens.

Suddenly in the night, there was a wolf–like cry of alarm. Everyone in the house woke up. Father threw on his clothes, picked up his gun, and went out.

The rest of the family crowded around the window to see what was happening. All except Mary. She heard Isaac say, "It's just a coyote." She tried to go back to sleep. She didn't want to think about little Wolf out in the woods.

In the bright light from the snow, Father saw
the coyote near the hen house. He fired his gun.
The coyote turned and quickly ran behind the
hen house. Father fired again. But the coyote
had disappeared over the hill.

Father went into the hen house to make sure
the chickens were all right. Then he carefully tied
the door tight. He was about to return to the
house when he saw something at his feet.

It was the wolf-pup, wagging his tail.

"So it was you who warned us!" said Father. He reached down and took the puppy in his hands and looked at him. "Brave little pup, aren't you? Not afraid of cold or coyotes. Maybe you will earn your keep after all!"

Father carried the puppy into the house. Everyone was waiting for him—everyone except Mary. When they saw the wolf-pup, they all got excited. Father held up his hand for them to be silent. He carried the pup into Mary's bedroom.

Mary looked up as her father came in. He put the wolf-pup down on the bed. "This little pup would like to get warm," he said.

Mary could hardly believe she wasn't dreaming. "Can I keep him?" she asked.

"I guess you can," her father answered gruffly. But he was smiling as he said it. "I think this wolf-pup *will* be able to earn his keep. He did us a real favor tonight by warning us about that coyote."

In the doorway of Mary's bedroom, Isaac and Jake and Sarah and Mother, holding Eva in her arms, all stood watching and smiling.

Mary held little Wolf in her arms. "I knew it all the time!" she said happily. "I knew something special would happen today. And little Wolf really is something special."

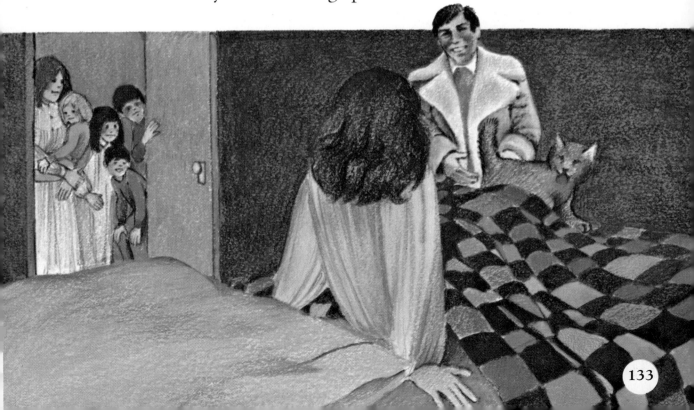

Mile 18 is a real place, even though it is too small to appear on a map of Canada. Mile 18 is 18 miles off the Alaska Highway. The closest town is Fort St. John, British Columbia, 45 miles away.

QUESTIONS

A. How was Mary's life different from your life?

B. How do you think little Wolf will earn his keep on the farm?

C. How do other animals earn their keep on a farm?

D. Why do you think Mary's family wanted to live in Mile 18 even though their life was not easy there?

E. How did Mile 18 get its name?

Vern

by GWENDOLYN BROOKS

When walking in a tiny rain
Across the vacant lot,
A pup's a good companion —
If a pup you've got.

And when you've had a scold,
And no one loves you very,
And you cannot be merry,
A pup will let you look at him,
And even let you hold
His little wiggly warmness —

And let you snuggle down beside
Nor mock the tears you have to hide.

A Glossary: How to Use It

Suppose you did not know the meaning of the word *moose*. Would you get very many clues from the other words in the sentence below?

We saw a **moose.**

Sometimes, even though you have read very carefully, the context doesn't give you enough help. You can still find out what the word means — if you have a glossary.

A **glossary** is sometimes found at the back of a book. The glossary is the part of the book where you can find the meanings of some of the words used in that book. There is a glossary at the back of this book. In it you will find meanings for some of the words used in this book.

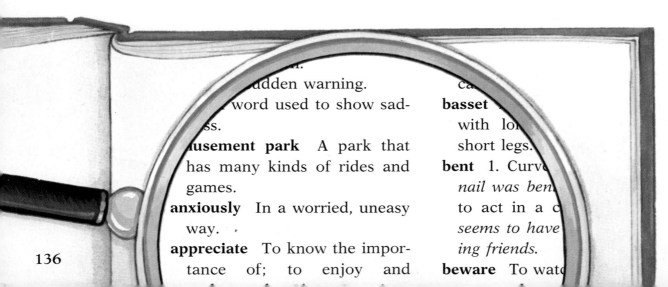

...dden warning.

...word used to show sad- ...ss.

...usement park A park that has many kinds of rides and games.

anxiously In a worried, uneasy way.

appreciate To know the impor- tance of; to enjoy and

basset ... with lo... short legs.

bent 1. Curv... *nail was ben...* to act in a ... *seems to have...* *ing friends.*

beware To wat...

You can easily find a word and its meaning if you know how to use a glossary. Most of the words in a glossary are listed as base words.

Base words are words without endings such as *s, ed,* or *ing.* If you were looking for the word *kneading,* you might have to look for the word *knead* without the *ing* ending.

The words in a glossary are listed in **alphabetical order.** The words that begin with *a* come first. Those that begin with *b* come next, and so on.

You can quickly find a word in the glossary if you know where to start looking. Suppose you were looking for the word *alarm.* You should look for it near the **front** part of the glossary because *alarm* begins with the letter *a.* Words that begin with a letter at the beginning of the alphabet are listed in the front part of the glossary.

If you were looking for the word *moment,* where would you start? You should start looking near the **middle** of the glossary because the letter *m* is near the middle of the alphabet. Words that begin with a letter near the middle of the alphabet are listed near the middle of the glossary. If you were looking for the word *turkey,* you would start looking in the **back** of the glossary. Why do you think you would start looking there?

Just below is part of a page from the glossary in this book.

---

grumble   **manage**

grumble To complain in a low grouchy voice.

ivy A hanging or climbing plant with green leaves.

There are two words in heavy black letters at the top of the glossary page. These words are called **guide words.** When you are looking for a word in a glossary, the guide words can help you find the right page. The guide word on the left tells you what the first word listed on that page is. The guide word on the right tells you what the last word on that page is. If the word you are looking for comes, in alphabetical order, between the two guide words, look for the word on that page.

FINDING WORDS IN A GLOSSARY

Below are four words. Find each of the words in the glossary at the back of this book. First decide if you should start looking in the front, middle, or back of the glossary. Then find the right page.

marshal   **torch**   **argue**   **camera**

Blue-Wings-Flying

by ELIZABETH WILLIS De HUFF

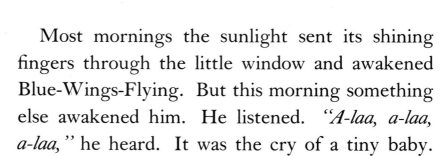

Most mornings the sunlight sent its shining fingers through the little window and awakened Blue-Wings-Flying. But this morning something else awakened him. He listened. *"A-laa, a-laa, a-laa,"* he heard. It was the cry of a tiny baby.

Blue-Wings-Flying wiggled out of his blanket and sat up. So-Oh (the Hopi word for *Grandmother*) was seated by the stove. Beside her was a basket of soft gray ashes. Gently she rubbed some ashes over the body of the tiny baby. Then she sprinkled the child with cornmeal. Tah-Tah (*Father*) was standing on a wooden chair, hanging up the baby's cradle.

Yu-Yu (*Mother*) was sitting on her rolled-up mattress. Blue-Wings-Flying ran to her, unable to ask the question.

"Yes," said Yu-Yu. "You have a baby sister."

The baby was wrapped in a blanket grown soft with much use. So-Oh handed the baby to Yu-Yu, who held her a moment for Blue-Wings-Flying to see. He touched the baby's face with his finger.

Suddenly Blue-Wings-Flying felt afraid. He thought of another baby, his little brother, who had died. He asked, "Will this baby sister stay with us?"

"Yes, she will stay if she keeps well and happy and has a pretty name." Yu-Yu smiled.

"I will play with this little sister to make her happy," said Blue-Wings-Flying. "And I will find a pretty name for her Naming Day."

"Yes," said Yu-Yu. "So-Oh and Tah-Tah and your uncles and aunts and cousins will all be watching for the prettiest thing they see or feel on this day of her birth. Then on her Naming Day, the one who has the nicest idea will be the one to name her."

"That will be many names. How will we know the best one?" asked Blue-Wings-Flying.

"The one that we begin to call her, after we hear all of them, will be her name," said Yu-Yu.

"I will go and look until I find a beautiful name," said Blue-Wings-Flying.

Yu-Yu gave him a pat on the shoulder. "Now you must eat. Tah-Tah will be waiting. You must help him fill the water jars at the spring."

Blue-Wings-Flying slowly shook his head. "I don't want to go, Yu-Yu. I want to look for a pretty name."

"You don't have to look far away for a name," said Yu-Yu. "There are pretty things everywhere for an eye to see. Keep your eyes open. Thoughts and eyes work together. Have beautiful thoughts and you see beautiful things."

Tah-Tah came in and picked up the big water jar. "Come, my boy," he said. "The burro and I are waiting."

Blue-Wings-Flying went outside. Tah-Tah was tying the jar onto one end of the blanket on the burro's back. He had already tied So-Oh's jar on the other side.

"*Ar-ray,*" Tah-Tah called to the burro. The jars swung back and forth as the burro headed up the steep path. The burro moved very quickly, and Blue-Wings-Flying followed at a half run. He frowned — there was no time to look for pretty things to name his baby sister.

Tah-Tah noticed and said, "Nothing will look pretty if you frown, my boy."

At one turn in the path, there was an opening in the high wall. At other times, Blue-Wings-Flying had seen blossoms of Indian paintbrush there. He stopped to look inside. As he did, Tah-Tah spoke.

"No need to look for flowers. They appear only when it rains, and no rain has come for many months. The flowering plants are dried up."

At the bottom of the hill, the burro went more slowly, eating dried grass here and there.

Blue-Wings-Flying sighed to himself. "I have kept my eyes open, and I am not frowning, but I cannot see a good name anywhere. Everyone will have a pretty name but me."

Suddenly the burro stopped, his eyes wide open with fright. He wheeled around and dashed away as fast as the bumping jars would let him go.

Tah-Tah and Blue-Wings-Flying looked to see what had alarmed the burro. It was a rattlesnake, winding itself into rings, one upon the other. Its lifted tail was shaking angrily. The rings on the tip of its tail rattled to warn them off.

Blue-Wings-Flying stood as if he had been turned into stone.

Tah-Tah whispered, so low that he could hardly be heard, "Don't move. Don't show that you are afraid. We must let the snake know that we are its brothers."

Blue-Wings-Flying could not help feeling afraid, but he stood very still. Not even his eyes moved from the rattlesnake. Tah-Tah stood still beside him.

The snake closed its mouth, lowered its tail, and straightened its body. Then it slipped away into the rocks and was gone.

After a few moments, Blue-Wings-Flying sighed with relief. Tah-Tah went to get the burro.

"There are pretty marks on the rattlesnake," thought Blue-Wings-Flying. "But a snake name might frighten a child."

When they reached the spring, they untied the jars from the burro. Tah-Tah said, "So-Oh's jar is lighter than ours. It is made of better clay. Take it and fill it with water."

His arms barely reaching around the big jar, Blue-Wings-Flying walked carefully to the spring. He lowered the huge jar into the water. The jar was so big that it was hard for him to get a good hold on it. Suddenly — *clink* — the jar slipped from his hands and struck the stone wall. Blue-Wings-Flying caught the jar. But a piece broke off and disappeared into the spring.

For a moment, Blue-Wings-Flying could not
move. His eyes filled with tears. So-Oh loved the
jar; it had belonged to her own grandmother.

Then he tipped the jar to fill it with water. A
ray of sunlight made a rainbow in the mist coming
up from the spring. Blue-Wings-Flying looked at
the rainbow but he did not think about it. His
thoughts were all about So-Oh and the sadness
she would feel when she saw the broken jar.

Tah-Tah had turned away to save his son from greater shame. But now Tah-Tah lifted So-Oh's jar and carried it to the burro. He gave Blue-Wings-Flying the other jar to fill, to show his trust. Then Tah-Tah put his hand on the boy's head. "There will be other jars. Things that break do not last forever." Together they reloaded the burro and began to climb the steep path.

So-Oh was cooking pancakes when they reached home. Blue-Wings-Flying watched her slowly shake her head as Tah-Tah brought in the water jars. Blue-Wings-Flying ran to her. "Your jar was heavy, So-Oh. It slipped and hit the spring wall."

So-Oh could not speak. She stood very still, looking at the broken jar. Finally she turned and went back to cooking pancakes. Blue-Wings-Flying knew she was sad. He knew, too, that she would not scold him. But he would feel better if she did.

Yu-Yu stood by the cradle and swung the baby. Blue-Wings-Flying ran over to Yu-Yu. She whispered, "I will weave a big basket. We will trade it in the village for a new jar for So-Oh."

"But it will not be an old jar," said Blue-Wings-Flying, trying to keep back the tears.

"The jar will be old for your sister when she is old like So-Oh," Yu-Yu said, smiling. Blue-Wings-Flying felt a little better.

Suddenly he wondered what time it was. He went to the window and peeked out. It was time for the sun to set. Blue-Wings-Flying hurried outside.

As always, the shining ball of sunlight slipped down behind the mountain tops, pulling behind it a great blanket of colors. Watching the sunset, Blue-Wings-Flying felt that he had forgotten something — something important, something he should remember.

That night Blue-Wings-Flying lay awake wondering what the sunset had tried to tell him. Then a picture came into his mind. He saw again the spring and the broken jar filling with water. He saw it clearly, and all at once he had a name for his baby sister. He longed to say it aloud, once, just to hear how it sounded. But it was a secret to keep until it was his turn to name the baby. Blue-Wings-Flying closed his eyes, the picture still in his mind. Soon he was asleep.

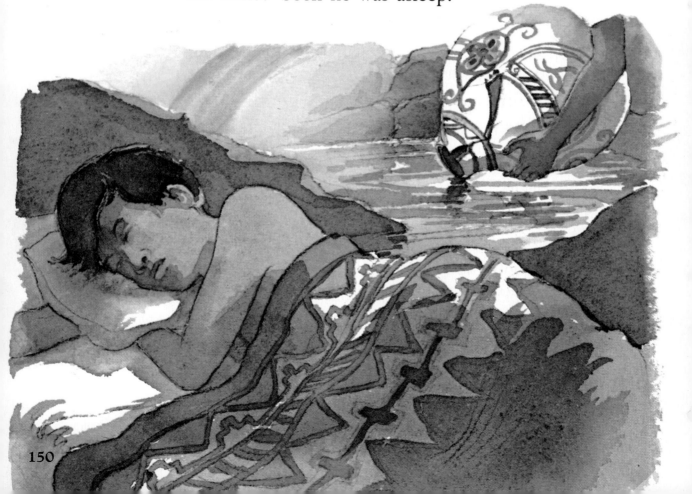

The next morning, some of his aunts and uncles and cousins came to help get ready for the Naming Day. So-Oh was spreading corn batter over a hot, flat stone. Blue-Wings-Flying liked to watch her peel the thin-as-paper bread off the flat stone and fold it into long flat sticks.

Tah-Tah came in with many heavy bundles of food from the trading store. Blue-Wings-Flying helped him unload. When they had finished, Tah-Tah turned to the boy. "This house is getting too crowded now. You had better go out and play."

Blue-Wings-Flying went out to find his friends, but he did not go far away from his own house. When he saw more people coming from many directions, he ran to go inside with them.

As soon as everyone was seated on rolled-up mattresses and sheepskins, So-Oh got up. She held an ear of white corn. Touching the baby's head with the corn, she said, "I name you Pink-Clouds-in-the-morning."

Blue-Wings-Flying looked around. He saw most of the people smile and nod their heads. "They like that name," he thought.

Tah-Tah took the ear of corn. He touched the baby's head with it. "I name you Singing-Corn-Leaves-in-the-wind," he said. Blue-Wings-Flying remembered the soft sound of wind blowing through the corn stalks by the river. It was a nice sound. Some of the visitors nodded.

Yu-Yu's cousin took the corn. "I name you Shining-Sun-on-a-bright-tin-can." A few visitors put their hands to their mouths to cover their smiles.

Another cousin said, "I name you Running-Chipmunk."

One by one, each person gave a name. Then it was the turn of Blue-Wings-Flying-in-the-sunlight. He was the last because he was the youngest.

Yu-Yu whispered, "Let the ear of corn touch like a butterfly." Blue-Wings-Flying nodded.

He touched the baby's head lightly and said, "I name you Rainbow-Mist-at-the-spring."

He looked shyly around the room. No one nodded. No one was smiling but Yu-Yu. So-Oh had a thoughtful frown on her face. Then they all stood up to eat. "Maybe they did not even hear my name," he thought.

Blue-Wings-Flying ate little. When the other children had finished, one of the girls said, "Come play." She pulled Blue-Wings-Flying by the arm and together they went outside, followed by the other children.

After a while, Blue-Wings-Flying slipped away. He wanted to be there to hear what the baby was being called.

Blue-Wings-Flying went into the house and saw that almost everyone had gone. So-Oh sat holding the baby. Yu-Yu came to take the baby, and as she lifted the tiny bundle, she said, "Come, little Rainbow-Mist. You must go back to your cradle."

So-Oh got up. "Good night, little Rainbow-Mist," she said.

In his happiness, Blue-Wings-Flying hugged himself and laughed out loud. He went to the cradle and touched his mother's arm. When she looked, he smiled and watched her smile back.

Blue-Wings-Flying peeked into the cradle and said softly, "Good night, little Rainbow-Mist."

QUESTIONS

A. Why do you think Tah-Tah turned away when Blue-Wings-Flying broke the jar?

B. Why do you think Tah-Tah wanted to show that he trusted Blue-Wings-Flying to fill the other jar?

C. Yu-Yu told Blue-Wings-Flying that he would see beautiful things if he had beautiful thoughts. Do you agree? Why or why not?

D. What happens in the story that shows that the Hopi people notice and care about the beautiful things in the world?

There Is Joy

translated by KNUD RASMUSSEN

There is joy in
Feeling the warmth
Come to the great world
And seeing the sun
Follow its old footprints
In the summer night.

There is fear in
Feeling the cold
Come to the great world
And seeing the moon
— Now new moon, now full moon —
Follow its old footprints
In the winter night.

156

The Duck in the Gun

by JOY COWLEY

For days the General and his men had been marching. Now they were all around the town and ready for the war.

The General called his Gunner.

"Is the gun in place?" he said.

"Yes, sir," said the Gunner.

"Is it aimed at the town?"

"Yes, sir," said the Gunner.

"Good," said the General. "Load it. When I give you the order, fire the gun."

"Very well, sir," said the Gunner, and he went away. But a little while later he came back. "Sir, we can't fire that gun."

"Why not?" shouted the General.

"Because we can't load it, sir."

The General grew red in the face. "Why can't you load it?" he shouted.

"Please, sir," said the Gunner. "There's a duck in the gun."

"A duck? In our gun?" The General jumped up from his chair.

"It has made a nest in there, sir."

"How dare it!" shouted the General. "It must go at once."

"I've tried, sir," said the Gunner. "But the duck won't come out. I think it is sitting on some eggs."

"Then I'll do something about it myself," said the General. "I'll show that duck it can't stop an army."

The General and the Gunner went out to where the gun had been set, aimed at the town.

"You mean the duck's right in there?" said the General.

"Yes, sir," said the Gunner. "I put my hand in but couldn't reach it."

The General looked down the gun and saw two small eyes looking back at him. "Here, dilly, dilly, dilly," he called. "Nice dilly."

The duck said, "Quack, quack," but didn't
move.

The General's face went red again. "Come
out, you!" he shouted.

There was another quack, but the duck
didn't stir from her nest.

"Please, sir," said the Gunner. "Could we
put some food at the end of the gun? If the
duck is hungry, it'll come out and eat."

"A very good idea," said the General. "Get
me some bread at once."

They put bits of fresh bread in the end of the gun, but still the duck would not come out.

The General stamped up and down. "To think that a duck could upset my plans," he said.

"There is something you can do, sir," said one of the men. "You can fire it with the duck inside."

"No, no, no," said the General. "We'll think of something else. I know! We'll borrow a gun."

The General picked up a white flag and marched into the town.

"Take me to your Prime Minister," he said to the town guards.

The guards led him through the streets to the Prime Minister's house. The General knocked on the door, and at once it was opened by the Prime Minister's daughter.

"Good afternoon," said the General. "Do you know who I am?"

"Oh, yes," said the girl. "I've seen your pictures in the paper. Won't you come in?" She turned away and called, "Father, here is the General to see you."

"How do you do?" said the Prime Minister.

"Not very well," said the General, shaking his head. Then he told the Prime Minister about the duck in the gun.

"I see," said the Prime Minister. "And you can't really fire the gun with the duck inside. What are you going to do about it?"

"Ah-hmmm," said the General. "That's why I came to see you. I was wondering if we could borrow a gun. I mean, it's not very fair if you have guns and we haven't."

"Oh, I agree," said the Prime Minister. "But you see, we have only one gun."

"Couldn't we share it?" said the General. "You could fire at us. Then we could take the gun and fire at you."

The Prime Minister laughed. "Oh, no. We can't let you have our gun. Besides, it is far too heavy to move."

For a while the General looked unhappy.

"Well, it looks as though you'll have to put the war off for three weeks," said the Prime Minister. "By that time the eggs will have hatched, and you will have your gun back."

The General shook hands with the Prime Minister. "That's fair enough," he said. "We'll forget about the war for three weeks."

When the General's men heard the news, they were quite pleased. They would have three weeks off. In fact, they were so pleased that they put food down the gun whenever the General wasn't looking.

But after one week, the General had another problem. He picked up his white flag and went to see the Prime Minister again.

"How are you?" said the Prime Minister.

"Not good at all," said the General. "The fact is, I'm running out of money. For a whole week my men have done nothing, and they want me to pay them for it."

"That *is* a problem," said the Prime Minister.

"I don't suppose you would let me borrow some money," said the General.

"No," said the Prime Minister. "I can't give men money for doing nothing. But I can pay them if they will work for me. See our town? It needs painting. In two weeks, your men could paint the whole town."

"What a great idea!" said the General. "Thanks very much. I'll tell my men at once."

This time the men were not so pleased. But when the General said he could no longer pay them, they agreed to work in the town.

Early next morning they put on old clothes and left the camp. As soon as the last man had gone, the General went out to look at the gun. The duck was still there, sitting on her nest and quacking to herself. The General looked over his shoulder to make sure that he was alone. He took some cake from his pocket, put it quickly down the gun, and then went back to his tent.

Every day the men went to work in the town. It was very quiet at the camp. Sometimes the General would look at the town through his glasses and watch the houses change color. Sometimes he visited the Prime Minister and his daughter and had tea in their garden. Sometimes he would just walk as far as the gun with a pocketful of bread.

Near the end of the third week, the eggs hatched. The General went by the gun and heard not only "Quack, quack," but also a tiny "Beep, beep, beep."

The General rang the alarm bell as loudly as he could. At once the men put down their paints and brushes and ran back to camp.

The General called, "Attention! The duck's eggs have hatched." He looked inside the gun.

"Here, dilly, dilly," he called.

Out popped a little head. It was the first duckling.

Very carefully, the General placed it on the ground. Then another duckling came out, and another, until eight of them were waddling around the General's feet. Last out was the mother duck. She looked at all the men and quacked loudly. Then she flew down beside her ducklings and marched them off across the grass.

"Three cheers for the duck," shouted the men, throwing their hats in the air. "Hooray, hooray, hooray!"

"Now we can use our gun again," said the General. "At last we can have a war."

The men stopped cheering. They became very quiet. They stood with their hats in their hands and looked down at the ground.

"Please, sir," said the Gunner. "We can't fire at that town. Just think what that would do to the fresh paint."

"Yes," said the other men. "We've worked for two weeks on those houses."

The General nodded. It did seem silly to blow up freshly painted houses. Besides, he had become rather fond of the Prime Minister's daughter.

"What will we do, then?" he said.

"You couldn't put the war off for good, could you, sir?" said the Gunner. "After we have finished painting the town, we can all go home."

The General thought for quite a long time. "All right," he said. "I'll go and tell the Prime Minister."

So that was the end of the war.

The men finished the painting in time to go to the wedding of the General and the Prime Minister's daughter. It was a big wedding with flowers and bells and a cake that had a white sugar gun on top.

Of course, the duck came. She and her eight ducklings were there to march behind the army band.

QUESTIONS

A. Why do you think the General wanted to have a war in the beginning?

B. Did anyone in the story seem to be upset because the war was put off? Why or why not?

C. What do you think might have happened if the duck had come out of the gun right away?

D. What parts of the story could really happen? What parts of the story would probably never happen in real life?

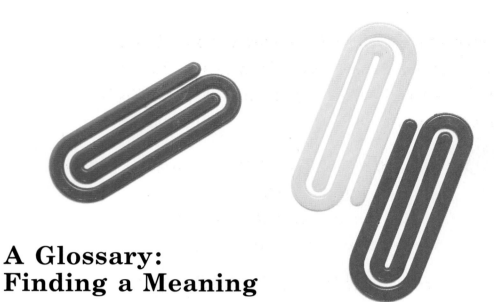

A Glossary:
Finding a Meaning

Do you know what *emergency* means? This word may be new to you. Do the other words in the sentence below give you any clues to the meaning of *emergency?*

This is an **emergency!**

When you can't get the meaning by using the context, you can check to see if the word is in the glossary.

Use what you have learned about glossaries to see if you can find the word *emergency.* Where would you look first — the front, middle, or back of the glossary? See if you can find the right page. Use the guide words to help you.

Once you have found the word in your glossary, you are ready to learn what it means. When you found the word *emergency* in the glossary, this is what you saw:

> **emergency** Something that happens suddenly and calls for quick action: *The doctor was called to the hospital to help in an emergency.*

The word you are looking for is in heavy black letters. The meaning is printed right after the word. What is the meaning given for the word *emergency?*

Sometimes, after the meaning, there is a **sample sentence.** This is a sentence using the word you are looking for. This sentence may give you more help in getting the meaning of the word. Read the sample sentence for *emergency.* How does it help you to better understand the meaning of the word?

Once you have read the meaning for the word, go back to the sentence where you first saw the word. Read the sentence again.

This is an **emergency!**

Does the glossary meaning make sense in this sentence? Do you understand what the sentence means?

Whenever you meet a word that you don't know the meaning of, you can usually get the meaning by yourself. First, use the context. If the context doesn't give you the meaning, look for the word in the glossary. When you find the word, read the meaning. Then go back to where you first saw the word. Read the sentence or sentences again. This time you should understand better what the word means.

FINDING A MEANING

Use the glossary at the back of this book to help you get the meaning of each word in heavy black letters.

1. Maria noticed that the door was left **ajar.**
2. They ran to the trees for **shelter.**
3. The wizard opened a bottle of strange-smelling **liquid.**
4. Jean is very **grumpy** when she wakes up.
5. Everyone helped during the **harvest.**

The Troll Bridge

by LILIAN MOORE

This is the Bridge
of the
Terrible Troll.
No one goes
by
without paying
a toll,
a terrible toll
to the Troll.

It's no place to
loll, to
linger or
stroll,
to sing or to
play.

So if ever you
ride
to the
opposite side,
be ready to
pay
the terrible troll —
I mean terrible toll —
to the Terrible Toll —
I mean Troll.

175

Sidewalk Story

by SHARON BELL MATHIS

Lilly Etta Allen was quite upset to learn that her best friend Tanya Brown was leaving her neighborhood. Mrs. Brown and her seven children were being put out of their apartment because they had no money to pay the rent. Already the marshals had come to take the family's things from the apartment. The marshals were piling the things on the sidewalk. Lilly Etta decided that she must try to do something to help Tanya.

Suddenly Lilly Etta had an idea. She had known a woman named Mrs. Ruth who had been put out of her apartment by mistake. She was then let back in, with the help of the police and the newspaper people. Lilly Etta decided to use the pay phone in the park to call the police and the newspaper, to see what could be done for the Brown family.

When Tanya and Lilly Etta got to the park, Tanya said, "Are you sure you can do it? Sound grown-up and everything?"

"Of course! That's nothing to do."

"Who you going to call first?"

"The police."

Lilly Etta put the money into the pay phone and dialed "0." The operator answered, "May I help you?"

"I want the police, please."

"Is it an emergency?" asked the operator.

Lilly Etta thought for a moment. "Yes, it is, please." She liked the way she said that.

"Police headquarters." The voice was gruff.

Lilly Etta put her mouth close to the phone. "I'm in trouble and you must come and stop it."

"What's the trouble? And what is your name?"

"Some men are taking my stuff and putting it on the sidewalk. If you come, they'll stop," said Lilly Etta.

"Are the marshals there?" the gruff voice asked.

"Yes, but —"

"If the marshals are there, there's nothing we can do. It's not a police matter."

"But I remember when —"

"Just a minute. How old are you?"

Lilly Etta didn't answer. The voice came again. "We would like to help, but there's nothing we can do. I think you'd better hang up the phone." There was a click and the phone was silent.

"He didn't even try to help," Lilly Etta said. "He didn't even try. He just wanted to know if the marshals were there."

Tanya said, "They have to make sure everything is out and the door is locked. Then they leave. Nobody guards the furniture. The marshals just bring the paper and wait around. The paper is the eviction notice. My mother was crying at first when they gave it to her."

Lilly Etta was thinking again. "We only have enough money to call the newspaper people." She dialed "0" for Operator again.

"May I have the number for the newspaper, please?"

"Which newspaper do you want?" asked the operator.

"The large paper that comes out at night."

There was silence for a moment, and then the operator gave her a number. Lilly Etta repeated the number out loud so that Tanya could help her remember it.

The money came back, and Lilly Etta put it into the phone again. She dialed the number carefully because she didn't want to make a mistake.

A man answered.

"May I speak to a reporter, please?" asked Lilly Etta.

"What kind of reporter do you want?"

"The kind that comes and takes pictures when people can't pay their rent and all their stuff is put on the sidewalk," answered Lilly Etta.

After a few clicking sounds, Lilly Etta heard another voice. It boomed, "City room. Frazier speaking."

"Something is wrong and we want you to help us. Can you?" asked Lilly Etta.

"I'm not sure. What's going on?"

"I didn't have any money to pay the rent because I had to buy food first, and now men are putting all my things on the sidewalk in a pile and everybody is looking. When Mrs. Ruth was put out, the police and the news people came and made them put it all back. And now we want you to come and make them put back all of Tanya's stuff. I mean Mrs. Brown's stuff. That's me. I'm Mrs. Brown."

"Where do you live, Mrs. Brown?" The voice wasn't booming any longer. It was quiet and gentle.

Lilly Etta told him Tanya's street and house number.

"I don't think we can stop it," said Mr. Frazier.

"Yes you can!" cried Lilly Etta. "Yes you can!"

There was no sound on the other end. Lilly Etta didn't want the reporter to hang up the way the police had, so she lowered her voice. "When you came for Mrs. Ruth, they had to put all her things back in the house."

Lilly Etta could tell that Mr. Frazier was laughing a little. "Who did you say you were?"

"The woman named Mrs. Brown who's in trouble," said Lilly Etta. "Her girl is standing right here, and we want you to come and stop them from putting her stuff out."

"I thought you said *you* were Mrs. Brown," said Mr. Frazier. "How old are you?"

Lilly Etta thought for a second and answered, "I'm fifty."

"Tell me about yourself," said Mr. Frazier.

Lilly Etta didn't know what to say. She whispered to Tanya, "He wants to know about me. What's he want to know about me for? That's silly!"

Mr. Frazier heard her. "It's not silly at all," he said. "I think you're very interesting. If you'll tell me who you really are, maybe I can help you. And maybe I can't. First you have to tell me your real name."

"Lilly Etta Allen."

"Where do you live, Lilly Etta Allen?"

Lilly Etta told him. Then she said, "Can you help?"

"We can't really stop an eviction. We report it and call attention only if something is wrong."

"But something *is* wrong," said Lilly Etta.

"I'm listening," said Mr. Frazier.

"Well, first, Mrs. Brown has seven children. She missed work when the little kids were sick, and she had to buy food with the rent money. So something *is* wrong. It's a mistake to put her out for that."

"That may be true, Lilly Etta, but it's not a real news story. It happens all the time." He stopped a moment. "The only thing different about this story is you. How old did you say you were?"

"Nine. But when my birthday comes I'll be ten, and then I'll get real gold earrings." She thought of how long she had been away from her house. "But maybe I won't, if I get in trouble. I got to get back home."

"Good luck," he said. "Maybe things will turn out all right for you and for Mrs. Brown."

"Thank you," Lilly Etta said sadly. She hung up the phone.

She had no way of knowing that the reporter held the phone to his ear for a long time.

A Crash of Thunder

Lilly Etta was still eating when Tanya called. "I'm going, Lilly Etta! I'm going!"

Lilly Etta's sneakers couldn't get her to the window fast enough. She slipped and almost fell. "Tanya! I'm coming outside!" she yelled to her friend.

Tanya called again, "A cab is waiting for us. I have to go. I can't wait for you!"

"Mamma, Tanya has to go get in a cab. Can I run downstairs and see her before she leaves? OK? Please? Please!"

"You go on, Lilly Etta. Louise Brown won't need me standing around looking. I guess I told her what I had to say already." Mrs. Allen's voice was quiet.

Lilly Etta watched her for a moment before she dashed out the door. Maybe her mother didn't want to say good-by again. But Lilly Etta did, and she had to hurry.

She whizzed down the stairs. She didn't stop until she was next to Tanya on the sidewalk.

Lilly Etta didn't feel strong any more. Tanya was really leaving.

"Don't go, Tanya," she cried. "Please don't go." Lilly Etta wanted to say, "You're my best friend. Nobody else except you." But she didn't.

"I have to go, Lilly Etta. I *have* to."

Lilly Etta was beginning to feel sick in her stomach. Why did Tanya's voice seem so far away?

"We're going to Cousin Helen's. But I don't want to. Every time we go over there, Steven and I end up fighting because he doesn't want anybody to touch his stuff. Now we'll be fighting forever!"

A woman came out to see what was happening. "Big deal," she grumbled. "Putting seven babies and a mother on the street. Don't make no sense." She touched Mrs. Brown. "Keep your head up, Brown. This isn't the end." She walked over to the pile and pointed to a highchair. "Babies on the street!"

Another woman came up to Mrs. Brown. "I'm going to do what I told you," she said. "My cousins have a house they've been thinking about renting. I'll see about it for you."

A man walked up to Mrs. Brown and handed her some money. "Take this money for the cab," he said.

"No." Mrs. Brown shook her head. But the man leaned in and gave it to the cab driver.

Mrs. Brown hugged the man. There were tears in her eyes.

"Grow stronger, sister," he said to her and walked away.

Everyone was talking, but Lilly Etta didn't want to talk any more. Tanya didn't either. Tanya sat close to the driver and stared at the steering wheel while Lilly Etta just stood on the sidewalk. There was nothing left to do or say.

The cab pulled away and moved slowly down the crowded street. Lilly Etta waved until the cab had disappeared. Then she ran back up to her apartment. She pushed the door open and banged it shut, which her mother didn't like. Then she ran to the front window and threw it open.

The crowd was moving away, and Lilly Etta was crying. "I'm going to stay up all night and watch their stuff on the street," she said to herself.

Later that evening, Lilly Etta looked down at the pile for the hundredth time. Everything was still in place. Except for some magazines. Pages and pages were flapping in the wind.

Wind?

"Where did the wind come from all of a sudden?" Lilly Etta wondered. It hadn't been windy all day. She saw that it was darker than it should be.

Lilly Etta looked up. The sky looked funny. Like rain. Rain!

"Rain!" she yelled to her mother. "I think it's going to rain. It's windy and everything, and the sky is black, and it's too dark outside." She could hardly say the words. "You think it's going to rain, Mamma? It's not going to rain, is it?"

"Now listen, Lilly Etta. Even if it does, there's nothing you can do about it."

"But Mamma, what about Tanya's stuff?"

"No more talking about it, Lilly Etta. No more. If it rains, it rains. Nobody can stop it. There's nothing you can do."

Nothing had worked. She hadn't helped Tanya at all. Lilly Etta fell asleep listening for rain.

But it was the crash of thunder that woke her up.

Lilly Etta lay very still. She wondered if she had really heard it. There was no sound now. She had to get to the window and see what was happening.

She got out of bed slowly. If she wasn't quiet, she would wake her brothers. She didn't make a sound as she tiptoed into the living room and opened the window.

She stuck her head out. The air was hot and
sticky. It was so black she couldn't see anything.
Then there was a flash of lightning across the sky.
The crash of thunder was so loud it seemed to
split the skies open.

"Oh!" Lilly Etta stood still. "*Oh!* It's going to
rain!" She almost said it too loud. She shut the
window fast but quietly.

Blankets in the Wind

Lilly Etta went back to her room, pulled on her raincoat over her pajamas, and slipped her feet into her sneakers. Then she tiptoed to the place where the towels and sheets and blankets were kept. She filled her arms with as many sheets and blankets as she could carry. Even some old baby blankets. "I hope this can cover all of Tanya's stuff. But if it rains too hard . . ." Lilly Etta didn't want to think about that. She was ready to go.

Her heart was pounding and her arms hurt as she walked down the hall, past her mother's bedroom, past — She heard her mother move. Lilly Etta waited until she could no longer hear a sound. "I've got to hurry," she thought as she stood at the dark front door.

The stairway was dark, and the steps squeaked loudly. Strange-sounding night squeaks.

Squeeeeeeeeeaaaaaaaaaaak!

Squeeeeeeeeeeeeeeeeaaaaaaaaaaaaaaaaak!

Lilly Etta heard laughter in one of the apartments she passed. And she almost ran into a cat. It made her feel like she was in a ghost story.

She and the bundle got to the ground floor, but she had a hard time opening the door. Then she almost fell down the outside steps.

Lilly Etta tried to spread the sheets and blankets over the pile.

It wouldn't work. She couldn't reach the top in some places. And when she threw a sheet or blanket up, the wind blew it off. Baby blankets were blowing all over the street, and she had to run for them.

The wind died for a few moments and nothing moved. The sheets and blankets were still. Lilly Etta thought of something.

Quickly she climbed on top of the pile. Once she slipped because things kept moving under her. Something was sticking her in the leg, and something else pressed against her stomach. It felt lumpy. But finally Lilly Etta found a good spot. It was on top and almost in the middle of the pile. It felt smooth and safe.

Lilly Etta stretched out her arms and legs to hold the sheets and blankets down. It took some moving around and some pulling every time the wind blew hard, but it worked.

The street was quiet. Lilly Etta began to get sleepy. She closed her eyes and whispered, "I'll just shut my eyes for a minute. When the wind stops, I'll sneak back in the house."

The wind kept blowing a blanket against Lilly Etta's face. It felt soft and feathery against her skin. Just like someone was gently touching her. Like her mother did when Lilly Etta was sick with a fever.

Lilly Etta was still thinking about this when she fell asleep.

Quite a Girl

"Oh, phooey!" was what Lilly Etta said when she woke up. "I'm in trouble."

The whole block was noisy and crowded, just the way it had been that afternoon. But this time there were police cars with great flashing lights.

Lilly Etta, wet and sleepy, was being lifted down from the pile. Over by the police cars she heard a man yelling, "Why didn't you bring that thing earlier? You people knew it was going to rain. But you wait for a crowd before you do something!"

Lilly Etta leaned against the man who had
lifted her from the pile. She sighed, "I was only
trying to help. I didn't want the rain to get on
Tanya's stuff."

"Well, Lilly Etta, I think you got what you
wanted," the man said.

"How come you know my name?" she said
sleepily.

"You told me," he said.

Lilly Etta knew she had never seen him before
in her whole life.

"Frazier, from the newspaper. Remember?"

"You came and brought all these people to help
Tanya?" asked Lilly Etta. It was raining hard
now, but people still crowded around. Lilly Etta
saw her mother coming down the stairs.

"Your phone call stayed on my mind all day," said Mr. Frazier. "And even though I was tired from working late tonight, I decided to come by and check out your story. Then I found you asleep on that pile in the rain. And I thought, 'This is really something!' So I called the newspaper and told them to get over here with cameras. You were really something to see — asleep in the rain, holding down those blankets to keep your friend Tanya's stuff dry."

"I never thought you'd come. I thought — " Lilly Etta saw her mother pushing through the crowd.

"People came because of you, Lilly Etta," said Mr. Frazier. "Look over there. Do you know what that is?"

"No, sir."

"That's a tarpaulin the police are covering Tanya's stuff with. No rain will get on it any more. I've got a friend named Bud at the First Street Police Station. He brought the tarpaulin when I called and told him the story." Lilly Etta liked Mr. Frazier's smile.

Lilly Etta's mother came up. "Lilly Etta Allen! Look at all my sheets and blankets and things on the ground and everywhere — and wet, too. And you're soaked! I can't sleep in peace without someone knocking on the door telling me what you did."

"Yes, ma'am."

"Yes, ma'am nothing!" Mrs. Allen said just as three reporters walked up. They had large camera bags that swung from their shoulders.

"Hey, Frazier," one of them said. "Is she the one who tried to cover the pile?"

"Yep!"

"How'd you happen to be here?" the reporter asked.

Mr. Frazier looked at Lilly Etta and smiled. "I'll let her tell you."

And Lilly Etta told them the whole story.

"Were you afraid?" asked another reporter.

"Of course not," she said as cameras flashed all around her. "All I was going to do was cover the pile and go back in the house, but the wind kept blowing and I had to hold everything down. The sheets and blankets and stuff." She didn't dare look at her mother.

The reporters took pictures of the pile and of Lilly Etta back up on it. And of Lilly Etta yawning. They had to take the pictures fast because it was pouring and everybody was getting wet.

Lilly Etta watched the police and the people and the flashing police-car lights and Mr. Frazier.

Mostly she watched her mother. "Now I'll *never* get real gold earrings for my birthday," she said almost to herself.

One of the reporters heard her. "How long have your ears been pierced?" he asked.

"A long time," Lilly Etta said. "All I do is get different straws all the time. Mamma burns the ends to get the germs off."

"When is your birthday, Lilly Etta?" Mr. Frazier asked.

"Oh, phooey. It's a long time away. It takes a long time to be ten."

"All right! Clear the street! Go back to your homes. It's all over. Clear the street!" Some older kids were yelling the police order all over again.

"Good night, Lilly Etta Allen," Mr. Frazier said. "You're quite a girl."

Lilly Etta's mother pulled her up the steps. "You just get on upstairs and get to bed," she said. "Do you know what *time* it is, girl?"

Lilly Etta was in bed, it seemed, one second after her mother opened the door. She didn't see her mother, later, standing by her bed with an armful of wet sheets and blankets. Mrs. Allen was smiling and shaking her head.

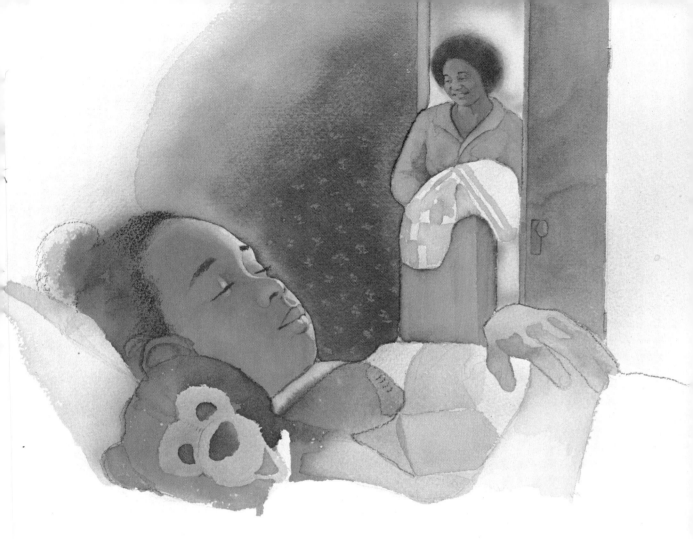

Every Single Earring

The morning and evening newspapers carried the story with pictures. Lilly Etta saw her face and the pile of blowing blankets and sheets.

That evening when the Allen family sat down to dinner, the doorbell rang. "I knew it," Mrs. Allen said. "Every time I sit down, someone rings!" She went to the door. "Who is it?" she called.

"Police."

"Oh, no! The police again. All because that child won't listen!" cried Mrs. Allen.

"No trouble this time. It's something good. We'd like to talk to Lilly Etta."

"Come in," said Mrs. Allen. "Lilly Etta!"

"Yes, ma'am?"

"Come into the living room. Hurry up. The police want to talk with you."

Lilly Etta was glad when she heard a familiar voice say, "And a reporter." It was Mr. Frazier. Now she could ask him a question that had been worrying her all day.

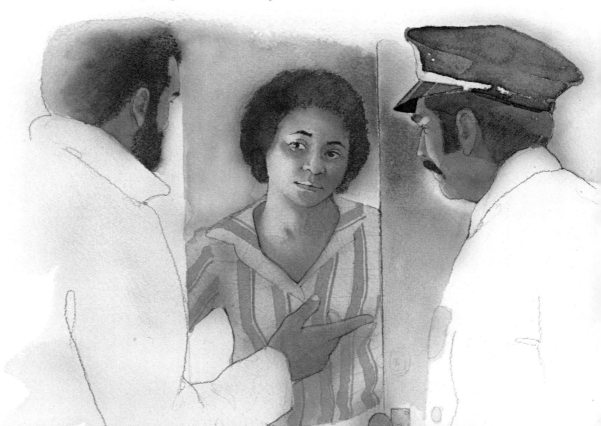

"I'm coming," she yelled. She came into the living room asking the question: "How come the police and the newspaper people didn't make the men come and put Mrs. Brown's furniture — you know, Tanya's stuff — back in the house like before when you came for Mrs. Ruth? All day long I've been looking outside and it's still there!"

"Hi, Lilly Etta. Everything's going great for Mrs. Brown. And *you* did it! Not the police or newspaper people."

"Phones have been ringing all day," the police officer added. "The owners of a warehouse will pick up Mrs. Brown's furniture tonight. They will store her things at no cost for a while. She's had a job offer, and a nursery school will keep her children at a small cost so she can work. And there's a larger apartment right here in the neighborhood which I understand she's going to rent."

"I'm so glad," Mrs. Allen said. "I'm so glad for that family." Mrs. Allen had tears in her eyes, just a little, but Lilly Etta could see them. Lilly Etta wasn't afraid. She knew her mother was crying because she was happy.

"And we have something for you, too, Lilly Etta. Something you want." Mr. Frazier handed her a box. "Open it," he said.

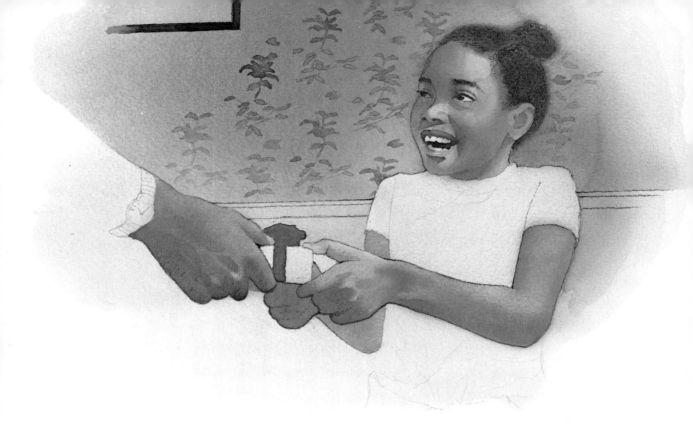

Lilly Etta did. And then she couldn't believe her eyes.

The box was filled with earrings.

Real gold earrings and some silver ones, too. Lilly Etta had never seen so many in her life.

"Oh, Mamma. Look!" Lilly Etta hugged the reporter. "Are all these mine? Can I keep them?"

The reporter smiled at her. "Yes," he said. "A lot of people thought a little girl like you shouldn't be without earrings. They called the paper saying, 'Where can I send some earrings for the little girl in pajamas with straws in her ears?'"

"People called the police stations, too," the police officer said. "So we collected all the earrings and brought them to you."

"Oh, my!" Mrs. Allen said.

"I can't wait till Tanya sees this box!" said Lilly Etta.

After the men had gone, Lilly Etta remembered the hug Mr. Frazier had given her as he left. And she found it hard to eat her dinner.

But that night Lilly Etta got up once again and stayed up a long time. She tried on every single earring.

The story you have just read is from the book, *Sidewalk Story,* by Sharon Bell Mathis. You can find out more about Lilly Etta and Tanya by reading the whole book.

QUESTIONS

A. What made Mr. Frazier call the police and the other reporters?

B. Although the Brown family had no money, what did they have that helped them get through this difficult time?

C. Why was Lilly Etta's mother angry when she first saw Lilly Etta on the pile?

D. How do you think Lilly Etta's mother felt at the end of the story about what Lilly Etta had done? Why do you think so?

E. Do you think everything will be easy now for Mrs. Brown and her family? Why or why not?

F. What do you think was the most important thing Lilly Etta did in the story? What makes you think that?

TWO FRIENDS

by NIKKI GIOVANNI

lydia and shirley have
two pierced ears and
two bare ones
five pigtails
two pairs of sneakers
two berets
two smiles
one necklace
one bracelet
lots of stripes and
one good friendship

What's in a Name?

Do you ever think about your name? In the story "Blue-Wings-Flying," it was very important to find a name for the new baby. To Blue-Wings-Flying and his family, the name had a special meaning. Did you know that almost all names have a meaning? The meanings of some names seem hidden because they come from old words or words from another language. But they do have a meaning.

Do you know anyone named *Leo*? *Leo* means "lion" in Latin, a very old language. The first person named Leo was probably strong like a lion. Maybe you know someone named *Sarah*. The name *Sarah* means "princess" in Hebrew, another very old language.

Last names have meanings, too. A smith is a "person who makes things." Can you guess how a person named *Goldsmith* got that name? Many years ago a person in that family may have made things from gold.

Many people were given names because of their jobs. Other people were given names because of where they lived. A person named *West* may have lived west of the village. A person named *Hill* probably lived in the hills.

You may not always understand the meaning of a name that comes from another language, but the meaning is there. The name *Taylor* comes from the word *tailor,* meaning a "person who makes clothes." Do you know any people named *Schneider* or *Snyder?* In the German language, these two names mean the same thing as the name *Taylor.*

If you would like to find out the meaning of your name, there are many books that can help you. It may take a little time to learn the meaning. But it is always fun to find out.

HI, I'M BILL BAKER!

HI, I'M ANN GARDNER!

TURNIPS   CARROTS

The Burning of the Rice Fields

by LAFCADIO HEARN

Far away in Japan, many years ago, lived good old Hamaguchi. He was the wisest man of his village, and the people loved and honored him.

Hamaguchi was a wealthy farmer. His farmhouse stood on a hillside high above the seashore. Down by the shore, and scattered up the hill, were the houses of his neighbors. Around his own house the ground was flat, like the top of a huge step in the hillside, and all about him stretched his rice fields.

It was the time of harvest. Hundreds of rice stacks lined Hamaguchi's fields. It had been a fine harvest, and tonight down in the village everyone was having a good time.

Hamaguchi sat outside his house and looked down into the village. He would have liked to join the other villagers, but he was too tired — the day had been very hot. So he stayed at home with his little grandson, Tada. They could see the flags and the paper lanterns that hung across the streets of the village, and see the people getting ready for the dance. The low sun lighted up all the moving bits of color below.

It was still very hot, though a strong breeze was beginning to blow in from the sea. Suddenly the hillside shook — just a little, as if a wave were rolling slowly under it. The house creaked and rocked gently for a moment. Then all became still again.

"An earthquake," thought Hamaguchi, "but not very near. The worst of it seems far away."

Hamaguchi was not frightened, for he had felt the earth quake many a time before. Yet he looked anxiously toward the village. Then, suddenly, he rose to his feet and looked out at the sea. The sea was very dark, and, strange to say, it seemed to be running away from the land.

Soon all the village had noticed how the water was rolling out. The people hurried down to the beach. Not one of them had ever seen such a thing before.

For a moment, on the hillside, Hamaguchi stood and looked. Then he called, "Tada! Quick — very quick! Light me a torch!"

Tada ran into the house and picked up one of the torches that stood ready for use on stormy nights. He lighted it and ran back to his grandfather. Quickly the old man grabbed the torch and hurried to the rice fields. Tada ran with him, wondering what he was going to do.

When they reached the first row of rice stacks, Hamaguchi ran along the row, touching the torch to each stack as he passed. The rice was dry, and the fire caught quickly. The seabreeze, blowing stronger, began to drive the flames ahead. Row after row, the stacks caught fire. Soon flames and smoke towered up against the sky.

Tada ran after his grandfather, crying, "Grandfather, why? Why?"

Had his grandfather gone mad? Why was he burning the rice that was their food and all their wealth? But Hamaguchi went on from stack to stack, till he reached the end of the field. Then he threw down his torch and waited.

The bell-ringer in the temple on the hill saw the flames and set the big bell booming. And, down on the beach, the people turned and began to climb the hill. If Hamaguchi's rice fields were afire, nothing would keep them from helping him.

First up the hill came some of the young men, who wanted to fight the fire at once. But Hamaguchi stood in front of the fields and held out his hands to stop them.

"Let it burn," he ordered. "Let it burn."

Soon the whole village was coming. Men and boys, women and girls, mothers with babies on their backs, and even little children came. Children could help pass buckets of water.

Still Hamaguchi stood in front of his burning fields and waited. Meanwhile the sun went down.

The people began to question Tada. What had happened? Why wouldn't his grandfather let them fight the fire? Was he mad?

"I don't know," cried Tada, for he was really frightened. "Grandfather set fire to the rice on purpose. I saw him do it!"

"Yes," cried Hamaguchi. "I set fire to the rice. Are all the people here now?"

The villagers looked about them. Then they answered, "All are here, but we do not understand —"

"Look!" shouted Hamaguchi, as loud as he could. He was pointing to the sea. "Look! Now do you think I have gone mad?"

All turned and looked toward the sea. Far, far out, where the sea and sky seem to meet, stretched a cloudy line that came nearer and nearer. It was the sea coming back to the shore. But it towered like a great wall of rock. It rolled more swiftly than a kite could fly.

"The sea!" screamed the people. Hardly had they spoken, when the great wall of water struck the shore. The noise was louder than any thunder. The hillside shook. A sheet of foam was dashed far up to where the people stood.

When the sea went back, not a house was left below them on the hillside or along the shore. The whole village had been swept away.

The people stood silent, too frightened to speak. Then they heard Hamaguchi saying gently, "That is why I set fire to the rice. . . . My house still stands, and there is room for many. The temple on the hill still stands. There is shelter there for the rest."

Then the people woke, as if from a dream, and understood. Hamaguchi had made himself poor to save them, and they bowed their foreheads to the ground before him.

QUESTIONS

A. What do you think caused the huge wave?

B. Why do you think Hamaguchi set fire to his fields rather than trying to get the villagers' attention another way?

C. What do you think Hamaguchi and the villagers will do now?

D. In what way did Hamaguchi show that he was wise?

What's the Matter with Carruthers?

by JAMES MARSHALL

One fall morning Emily Pig and her friend Eugene were taking a stroll in the park.

"What beautiful weather," said Emily. "I'm sure we are going to meet some of our friends here today."

"That would be very nice indeed," said Eugene. "It's such fun to bump into friends and have a little chat."

And sure enough, they came upon their old friend Carruthers, all bundled up and sitting alone on a wooden bench. He was gazing at the falling leaves.

"Good morning, Carruthers," they called out in their most cheerful voices.

"Good morning," said Carruthers. But his voice was far from cheerful. It was the kind of "Good morning" that really means "Don't bother me. I want to be left alone."

"I'm worried about Carruthers," whispered Emily to Eugene. "He hasn't been himself lately. He's so grumpy and unpleasant."

"It's not like Carruthers to be unpleasant," Eugene whispered back. "He always has a kind word for everyone."

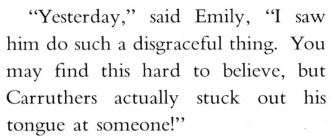

"Yesterday," said Emily, "I saw him do such a disgraceful thing. You may find this hard to believe, but Carruthers actually stuck out his tongue at someone!"

Eugene was shocked. "That doesn't sound like Carruthers. He has always had such lovely manners."

"But that's not all," said Emily. "The children in the park are complaining. It seems that Carruthers took away their ball."

"Oh, no!" exclaimed Eugene. "I just can't understand it. It is certainly not like Carruthers to be mean. He has always been so fond of children."

Leaving Carruthers to sit alone on his bench and gaze at the falling leaves, Emily and Eugene continued their stroll through the park.

"There must be something that we can do to lift Carruthers' spirits," said Emily. "And we had better do it soon. If Carruthers continues to act the way he has been acting, he won't have any friends left."

"That's very true," said Eugene. "No one likes a grouch."

And so the two friends sat together on a large rock and thought long and hard.

"Well," Eugene began, after a long pause. "Whenever I'm in a grouchy and unpleasant mood, I always listen to beautiful music. In no time at all I feel much better. And I'm sure that I'm much more pleasant to be around."

"That gives me an idea," said Emily. "Come with me."

The two friends hurried home, but in a few minutes they were back in the park with their musical instruments. Emily was carrying her tuba. Eugene had his tambourine.

"What a good idea," said Eugene. "When we smooth Carruthers' rumpled nerves with our beautiful music, he'll be his old friendly self again. I'm sure that he'll be so grateful."

They came upon Carruthers still sitting in the same place, still gazing at the falling leaves. And ever so quietly they tiptoed up behind him.

Emily placed the mouthpiece of her tuba to her lips. She puffed up her cheeks and began to play, softly at first and then quite loudly. Eugene tapped on his tambourine.

"*Um-Pah Um-Pah Tap Tap. Um-Pah Um-Pah Tap Tap.*" It sounded something like that.

But Carruthers was not impressed. Instead of listening to the music, he put his paws to his ears. "That is the most awful noise I have ever heard in my life!" he growled.

And he promptly got up and walked away.

Emily Pig and Eugene looked at each other. "Maybe we should have practiced more," said Eugene.

"No," replied his friend. "Some bears just don't and never will appreciate good music."

Emily set her tuba on the bench and sat down beside it. "But just because we could not improve Carruthers' mood with our music, that does not mean that we should give up. We must think of another way."

"Yes," replied Eugene. "We must not give up."

So once again they thought long and hard. "Whenever I am in a grumpy mood," said Emily, "I always have a little snack. I'm sure that a tasty snack would be just the thing for Carruthers. Maybe he hasn't been getting enough to eat lately. Why don't we invite him to lunch for honey cakes and tea? You know how fond bears are of honey cakes."

"What a clever idea," said Eugene. "Let's go to your house right away. We'll send Carruthers an invitation to come to lunch."

Emily and Eugene Try Harder

Carruthers was in an even grouchier mood when he came home from the park and found the invitation to lunch waiting for him. Certainly he was in no mood to go visiting — but what bear could turn down honey cakes? So of course he went.

At Emily's house Carruthers was given the very best chair. Emily poured the tea, and Eugene brought out the honey cakes.

"It's another beautiful day, isn't it?" said Emily, trying to start a friendly conversation.

"Not really," said Carruthers.

"You must enjoy strolling in the park," said Eugene.

"Not especially," said Carruthers.

"My, how lovely your fur looks today, Carruthers," said Emily.

"I've never cared for it," said Carruthers.

Emily and Eugene couldn't think of anything more to say — Carruthers was so determined to be unpleasant. And so the tea party continued in silence, except for the sound of Carruthers munching on honey cakes and drinking tea.

When the cake dish and the teapot were both empty, Eugene tried again. "Carruthers, you certainly must like Emily's honey cakes. You've eaten all twelve dozen of them."

"They were very tasty," said Carruthers. "Thank you for inviting me, but I must leave now. Stuffy in here."

"Yes, it is stuffy," said Emily. "Why don't we all go for a walk in the fresh air?"

"I don't like walking," said Carruthers.

"Then why don't we all go for a drive?" said Eugene.

"A wonderful idea!" exclaimed Emily. "I'm sure the change will do wonders for Carruthers."

And before Carruthers could say anything at all, he found himself all bundled up again and sitting in the back seat of Emily's traveling car.

Very soon the three friends were sailing through the open countryside.

"There's nothing like a drive in the country to cheer the spirits," called out Eugene.

"The countryside gives me hay fever," was all Carruthers would say.

Not far down the road they passed a large sign.

COME TO THE AMUSEMENT PARK
CLOSING SOON

"Ah," said Emily.

"Ah," said Eugene.

"Ugh," said Carruthers. "I hate amusement parks."

But Emily and Eugene paid no attention, no attention at all. "Rides and games are just what Carruthers needs," whispered Eugene.

"Yes," said Emily. "We are going, and that is that."

When they got to the park, Carruthers asked to stay in the car. But Emily would have none of that. "Nonsense, Carruthers! You must not be a bad sport."

Carruthers had never been good at arguing, especially with Emily. So Carruthers went into the amusement park. And he rode all the rides and played all the games that Emily told him to play.

But nothing seemed to improve his mood. He didn't smile even once — not even on the Ferris wheel, which had always been his favorite ride. He grumbled all through the fun house. And even after Carruthers had won eight lovely prizes, he was still the grouch he had been all day. "I think it's time to go home," he said. "I'm not having a good time."

Emily and Eugene were so discouraged. "I was sure this would work," said Emily. "It seems to me that we have tried just about everything, and Carruthers hasn't improved one little bit."

"Yes," said Eugene. "I suppose there is nothing to do but take Carruthers home."

On the way home no one spoke.

When they pulled up in front of Carruthers' little house, Emily had one last idea. "Carruthers," she said, "just look at all those leaves in your front yard. What a messy housekeeper you are! I really think we should help you rake some of them up before evening."

Now this was an idea that Carruthers did not like at all. Raking leaves in the late afternoon was not exactly his idea of fun. But he knew that Emily was going to have her way again. And he went off to find three rakes and a basket.

"I don't see why we should help Carruthers rake his leaves," said Eugene to Emily, "after all we have done for him today."

But Emily had made up her mind. "Sometimes keeping very busy is a good way to get out of a grumpy mood," she explained.

"We might as well give it a try," sighed Eugene.

When Carruthers returned, the leaf rakers set to work. Emily and Carruthers raked leaves into the basket. Eugene emptied the contents onto a pile he had started.

Very soon the pile was quite high.

"If we hurry," said Emily, "we will be finished in time for supper."

But Carruthers was already beginning to slow down.

He started to yawn — a small yawn, which he covered with his paw, to be polite.

Then a much bigger yawn.
But then — a great big bear yawn.

And without a word of warning, Carruthers plopped headfirst into the huge pile of leaves.

"Oh, my!" cried Eugene. "What in the world has happened?"

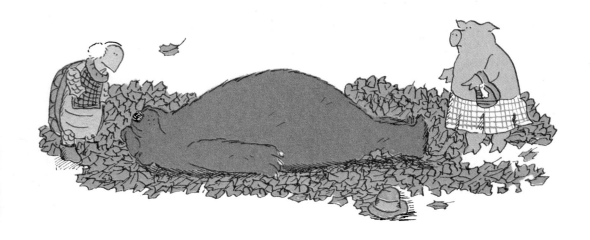

The two friends quickly cleared away the pile of leaves and uncovered Carruthers.

"He's asleep!" they exclaimed.

"So that is why Carruthers has been such an awful grouch lately," said Emily. "Why didn't we think of this before? He forgot that it was time for his long winter's sleep."

"Of course," said Eugene. "Carruthers should have been tucked away in bed days ago. No wonder he has been so impossible to be around."

"There is no use waking him now," said Emily. "He'll be asleep for the rest of the winter. It's up to us to get him into bed."

"That will be the hardest job yet," said Eugene.
But after a lot of huffing and puffing they managed to lift the sleeping Carruthers, who was just beginning to snore, into a small wagon and pull it into the house.

When they got to Carruthers' bedroom, they huffed and puffed again and ever so slowly put Carruthers under the heavy winter covers. Emily pulled his nightcap down around his ears. Eugene set the alarm clock for spring and drew the shades.

"Good night, Carruthers," whispered Emily, giving him a kiss on the cheek. "Sleep tight. And we'll see you in the spring when you will be your old sweet self again."

QUESTIONS

A. Why do you think Emily and Eugene were so determined to get Carruthers out of his bad mood?

B. Why didn't Emily and Eugene's ideas help Carruthers get out of his bad mood?

C. Did you guess what was wrong with Carruthers before the story ended? If so, what clues helped you? What fact about bears could have helped you guess?

D. Think about the last three stories you have read, "Sidewalk Story," "The Burning of the Rice Fields," and "What's the Matter with Carruthers?" What ideas about friends were the same in all three stories?

Autumn Leaves

by AILEEN FISHER

One of the nicest beds I know
isn't a bed of soft white snow,
isn't a bed of cool green grass
after the noisy mowers pass,
isn't a bed of yellow hay
making me itch for half a day —
but autumn leaves in a pile *that* high,
deep, and smelling like fall, and dry.
That's the bed where I like to lie
and watch the flutters of fall go by.

What's Wrong?

Can you tell what's wrong with this picture?

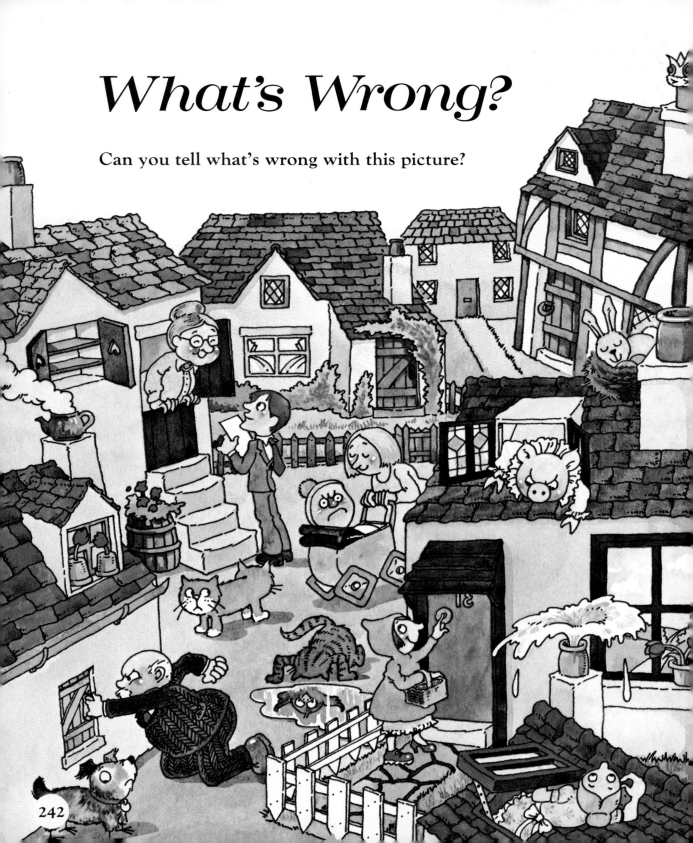

Books to Enjoy

My Friend Fish by Mamie Hegwood

A boy catches a fish at day camp and takes it home in a bucket to keep as his friend.

Fiona's Bee by Beverly Keller

Shy Fiona finds a funny, new way to make friends when she saves a drowning bee.

The Cuckoo's Reward by Daisy Kouzel

A Mexican folk tale tells how the cuckoo lost the beautiful colors of her feathers.

Garbage Delight by Dennis Lee

This is a lively collection of new nonsense poems by a prize-winning Canadian poet.

Elizabeth Catches a Fish by Jane Resh Thomas

On her seventh birthday, a girl's present from the family is a fishing trip with Dad.

Rosie and Michael by Judith Viorst

A girl and a boy share their good times and their bad times in this story of friendship.

Spinners

MAGAZINE THREE

Contents

MAXIE

by MILDRED KANTROWITZ

Maxie lived in three small rooms on the top floor of an old brownstone house on Orange Street. She had lived there for many years, and every day was the same for Maxie.

Every morning, seven days a week, every morning at exactly seven o'clock, Maxie raised the shades on her three front windows. Every morning at exactly 7:10, Maxie's large orange cat jumped up onto the middle windowsill and stretched out in the morning sun.

At 7:20, if you were watching Maxie's back window, you could see her raise the shade to the very top.

Then she uncovered a bird cage. Inside the cage was a yellow canary. The canary sang as it waited for its water dish to be filled, and it always was, if you were still watching, at 7:22.

At 8:15 every morning, Maxie's door opened with a tired squeak. Maxie's old, leather slippers made slapping sounds as she walked down the four flights of stairs to the front door. Outside the front door were the bottles of milk. Maxie always tried to hold the door open with her left foot while she reached out to get her milk.

But every morning it was just a little too far for her to reach. The door always banged shut and locked behind her.

So, at 8:20 every morning, Maxie rang the bell marked "Superintendent." The superintendent, whose name was Arthur, would open the door for Maxie and let her in with the milk.

Only Maxie and the man at the corner store knew what she ate for breakfast, but everyone knew she drank tea. At 8:45 every morning, they could hear the whistling of her tea kettle.

How Maxie loved that whistle! She loved it so much that she let it sing out for one full minute. Dogs howled, cats cried, and babies screamed. But everyone knew that when the whistle stopped, it would be 8:46. And it always was.

The letter carrier knew all about Maxie's mail. He knew that she had a sister in Chicago who sent her a Christmas card every year. He also knew when Maxie planted the flowers in her window boxes because every spring he brought her seed catalog. Then a few weeks later he brought packages of seeds.

Every morning at nine o'clock, Maxie walked down the stairs for the second time in her leather slippers. She went outside with her small bag of garbage. Then she came back in and waited for the letter carrier. She walked slowly past him, watching him put mail in the boxes for the other people who lived in the house.

Then she climbed the four flights of stairs again, resting at each landing. When she got to the top, Maxie went into her apartment. The door closed after her with the same tired squeak.

One afternoon at 1:05, just as she did every afternoon at 1:05, Maxie moved the bird cage with the yellow bird in it to the front windows. It was shady and cool there now.

The large orange cat moved to the back window and stretched out there, soaking up the sun that matched the color of its fur.

"You're perfectly happy just lying there, day after day," Maxie said to her cat. "All you ever want to do is move from one windowsill to the other and watch the world go by. You don't need anyone, and no one really needs you. But you don't seem to care." Maxie turned away from the window. "I care," she said sadly. "I'm not a cat. But I might as well be."

Maxie felt very tired, and she went to bed.

That was Monday.

On Tuesday morning at seven o'clock, the three shades on Maxie's front windows and the one on her back window stayed down. At 7:10, the large orange cat was still asleep at the foot of Maxie's bed. And at 7:30, the canary did not sing. That morning no one heard the sounds of Maxie's leather slippers on the stairs.

Her tea kettle was filled with empty silence.

At nine o'clock, the letter carrier came with the daily mail. He had a seed catalog for Maxie, and he waited for her to come down the stairs. Since she didn't come, and this was most unusual, he decided to take the catalog to her door.

He climbed the four flights of stairs. He knocked and waited. There was no sign of Maxie.

At 9:03, Mr. Turkle who lived on the third floor came hurrying up the stairs. At 9:05, Mr. and Mrs. Moorehouse got there from across the street. At 9:07, Mrs. Trueheart came over from next door. Susie Smith came up at 9:10 with her two brothers.

The family on the second floor made it by 9:13. Then came Arthur, the superintendent.

By 9:17, there were seventeen people, three dogs, and two cats, all waiting for Maxie to open the door. And when she didn't, they all went in. They found Maxie in bed.

More people came up the stairs. Someone called a doctor. By the time he got there, there were forty-two grownups and eleven children in Maxie's small living room.

When the doctor came out of Maxie's bedroom, he shook his head sadly. "Maxie isn't really sick," he said. "She's lonely. She doesn't feel loved. She doesn't feel that anyone needs her."

No one said anything for a minute. Then suddenly Mrs. Trueheart got up and walked right past the doctor and into the bedroom. "Maxie!" she shouted angrily. "You let me down. You and that singing bird let me down! Every morning when I wake up and hear that bird, it's my job to

wake my husband. He should be at the corner diner early in the morning, but he's still asleep. Why, there must be seventy-five people at that diner right now, waiting for their breakfasts. They'll all have to go to work on empty stomachs — all because of you and that yellow bird!"

Everyone else crowded into the bedroom. Maxie sat up and listened to what they had to say.

"I couldn't go to school this morning," Susie Smith said. "I missed my bus because I didn't hear your tea kettle whistle."

"The school bus never came this morning," said Mr. Turkle, the bus driver, "because I didn't wake up in time. I never heard Sarah Sharpe's footsteps on my ceiling."

Sarah Sharpe was a nurse who lived just above Mr. Turkle. There were a lot of people waiting for her right now at the hospital. She always got up when she heard Maxie's door squeak.

Mr. and Mrs. Moorehouse both had very important jobs, and they had missed their train that morning. Their alarm clock was Maxie's window shade.

Arthur said he hadn't swept the front steps that morning. He overslept because Maxie didn't ring his bell. He hoped no one would complain.

The people all talked about it and decided that there must be about four hundred people who needed Maxie — every morning.

Maxie smiled. She got out of bed and made a pot of tea. In fact, she made five pots of tea.

Each time the kettle whistled, dogs howled, cats cried, and babies screamed. Maxie listened and thought about how many people were being touched by these sounds — her sounds. By 9:45 that morning, Maxie had made tea for everybody, and she was so pleased.

QUESTIONS

A. Why did people depend so much on Maxie's sounds to wake them up?

B. What were some of the things Maxie did at exactly the same time every day?

C. Why do you think Maxie was lonely?

D. Do you think Mrs. Trueheart and the other neighbors were really angry with Maxie? Why or why not?

E. Do you think Maxie's neighbors had come to visit her before? Why or why not? Do you think they will come back to visit her now? Why or why not?

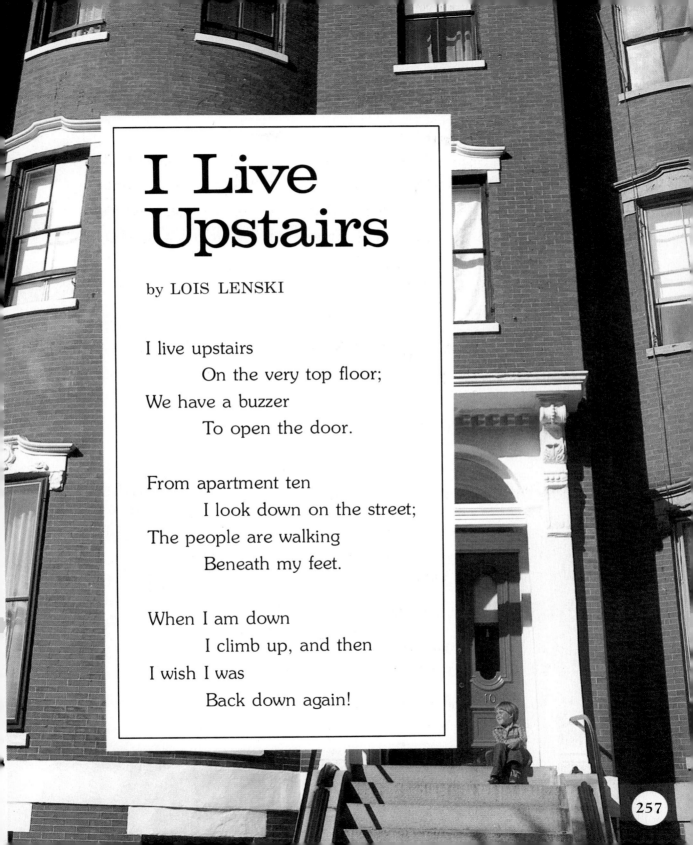

I Live Upstairs

by LOIS LENSKI

I live upstairs
    On the very top floor;
We have a buzzer
    To open the door.

From apartment ten
    I look down on the street;
The people are walking
    Beneath my feet.

When I am down
    I climb up, and then
I wish I was
    Back down again!

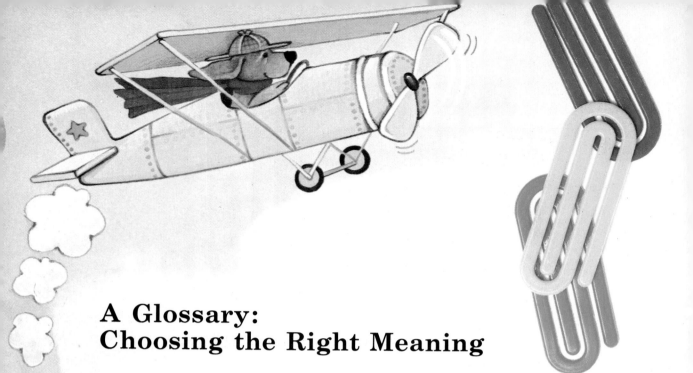

A Glossary:
Choosing the Right Meaning

You know that many words have more than one meaning. Read this sentence and think about the meaning of *flight*.

What airplane **flight** is he taking?

Now read the next sentence. Is the meaning for *flight* the same or different from the meaning in the sentence above?

Her apartment is one **flight** up.

You probably knew those two meanings for the word *flight*. But sometimes you may see a familiar word with a meaning that you do not know. The meanings you *do* know for the word don't make sense with the other words in the sentence. If the context does not give you enough help, you may need to use your glossary. Suppose you came to this sentence:

We saw a **chat** fly by.

The meaning of *chat* in this sentence is very different from the usual meaning. The other words in the sentence do not give you much help. If you looked up the word in a glossary, this is what you might find:

chat 1. A friendly, relaxed talk or conversation. 2. A North American songbird with a yellow breast.

You have probably noticed that there are two different meanings given for the word *chat*. Each meaning is numbered. Which meaning do you think would make the most sense with the other words in the sentence?

Sometimes you may come to a word that is not familiar at all. When you look up the word in the glossary, you might discover that it has more than one meaning. As you read each meaning, think about the context in which you first saw the word. Decide which meaning would make sense in that context.

Sometimes you may not be able to find a word in the glossary. A glossary lists just some of the words used in that book. If you cannot find a word in the glossary, you can look for it in a dictionary.

A **dictionary** is a book that gives the meanings for many, many words. A dictionary is very much like a glossary. The words are listed in alphabetical order. There are guide words on each page to help you find the word. One or more meanings for each word are given.

Whenever you need help with the meaning of a word in this book, check the glossary first. If you find the word, read the meanings and choose the one that makes sense with the context. If you can't find the word in the glossary, check in a dictionary.

CHOOSING THE RIGHT MEANING

Use the glossary at the back of this book to help you choose the right meaning for each word in heavy black letters.

1. Bill wore blue pants and a **canary** shirt.
2. Mrs. Moore plays **squash** every day.
3. We laughed as we watched the kitten **stalk** the fallen leaf.
4. Bob seemed to have a **bent** for getting into trouble.
5. The sailor liked to tell old **yarns** about his adventures at sea.

Anansi
the African Spider

by BARBARA WINTHER

The spiderman is a well-known character in African folk tales. Anansi is the name given to him by the Ashanti people of Ghana. Anansi is a sly, clever spider, and is often full of tricks.

Setting: An African forest

Characters:

First Storyteller	**Anansi,** *the spiderman*
Second Storyteller	**Crocodile**
Nyame, *the sky-god*	**Monkey**

First Storyteller: We are storytellers from an Ashanti village in Africa. We are going to tell you a story about Anansi, the spiderman.

Second Storyteller: Although that sly, clever Anansi is small, he can often outwit larger, stronger animals.

First Storyteller: The story we will tell is called "How Anansi Brought the Stories Down."

(*As the play begins,* **Nyame,** *the sky-god, is sitting in his home in the sky.* **Anansi** *is climbing up to visit* **Nyame.**)

Second Storyteller: It all happened long ago in Africa. Anansi thought it might be fun to tell stories in the evening.

First Storyteller: But Nyame, the sky-god, was the owner of all the stories.

Nyame: Here comes Anansi, the spiderman, climbing into my sky.

Anansi: Good day to you, sky-god.

Nyame: All my days are good, Anansi.

Anansi: But of course. It is only we poor earth creatures who have bad days.

Nyame: I'm not going to change that. If that's why you've come, go home.

Anansi: No, I'm here for another reason. I want to buy your stories.

Nyame (*Thundering*): What? Buy my stories? You dare to climb to my sky and ask me to sell you my stories? Great kings have tried to buy them. My stories are not for sale.

Anansi (*Sweetly*): Don't be angry with me, sky-god. I'm just a little spider trying to make my way in life. Isn't there any way I might talk you into giving up your stories?

Nyame (*Growling*):   What a bother you are!

Anansi: Why? Because I don't give up easily?

Nyame: Oh, all right, spiderman. If you can show me a crocodile with no teeth, an empty hornets' nest, and a quiet monkey, I'll give you my stories.

Anansi: Sky-god, you know that is impossible.

Nyame: But if you're as clever as some say, you can make it possible. Now go away. I must plan the weather for next week.

Anansi (*Climbing down*):   A crocodile with no teeth, an empty hornets' nest, and a quiet monkey. That will take some doing.

(***Anansi*** *sits as **Crocodile** enters.*)

Crocodile (*Opening mouth wide*): Hungry! Hungry! I'm so hungry I could eat anything.
(*Crocodile peers around for food. Anansi watches thoughtfully.*)

Anansi (*Aside*): I have an idea!

Anansi (*Calling to Crocodile*): Say, Crocodile, I know where you can get a good meal.

Crocodile (*Hurrying to Anansi*): Where? Where?

Anansi (*Pointing*): Over there.

Crocodile: I don't see anything but a big green rock.

Anansi: I see a plump, tasty frog that looks like a rock.

Crocodile: Yum, yum! A plump, tasty frog! I see it now. That frog is trying to trick me into thinking it is a rock.

Anansi: Why don't you sneak up quietly on that rock — I mean frog — and open your mouth wide? Then snap your teeth down just as hard as you can.

Crocodile: That's just what I'll do. Yum, yum! (*Crocodile sneaks toward rock as* **Anansi** *watches. Sound of a loud crunch is heard, followed by scattered pings.*)

Crocodile (*Shouting*): Ouch! That's the worst frog I've ever eaten!

Anansi: Aha! (*Calling up to* **Nyame**) Did you see that, sky-god?

Nyame (*With a thundering laugh*): Yes, Anansi. Greed broke the crocodile's teeth. Now find an empty hornets' nest.
(***Anansi** looks around.*)

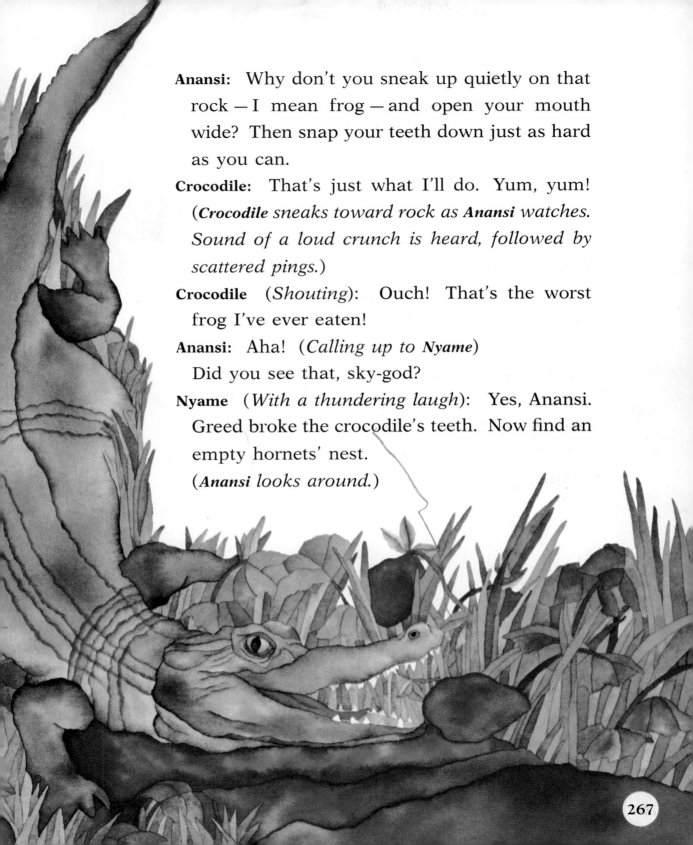

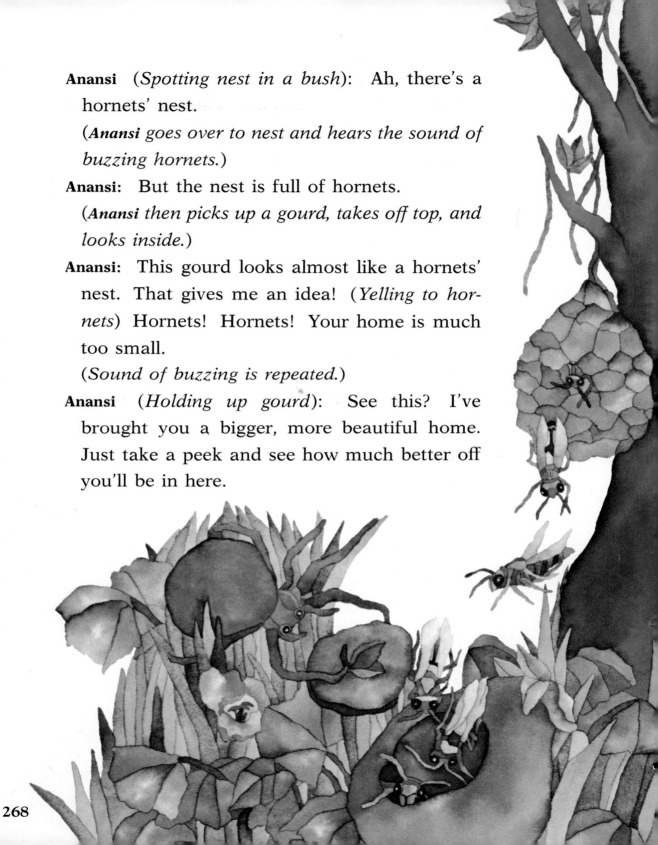

Anansi (*Spotting nest in a bush*):   Ah, there's a hornets' nest.

(***Anansi*** *goes over to nest and hears the sound of buzzing hornets.*)

Anansi: But the nest is full of hornets.

(***Anansi*** *then picks up a gourd, takes off top, and looks inside.*)

Anansi: This gourd looks almost like a hornets' nest. That gives me an idea! (*Yelling to hornets*) Hornets! Hornets! Your home is much too small.

(*Sound of buzzing is repeated.*)

Anansi (*Holding up gourd*):   See this? I've brought you a bigger, more beautiful home. Just take a peek and see how much better off you'll be in here.

(*Buzzing sound continues. **Anansi** watches hornets enter gourd, one by one. He suddenly bangs down top and buzzing sound stops.*)

Anansi: Aha! (*Calling up to **Nyame***) Did you see that, sky-god?

(***Anansi** holds up the real hornets' nest which is now empty.*)

Nyame (*Laughing as before*): Yes, Anansi. Dissatisfaction emptied the hornets' nest. Find a quiet monkey and all my stories are yours.

Anansi: This is going to be the hardest job of all.

(***Monkey** enters, leaping from tree to tree.*)

Monkey: Chitter, chitter, chatter. Look how pretty I am. Chitter, chitter, chatter. What a perfectly gorgeous monkey I am.

Anansi (*Aside*): I have an idea.

 (*Sighs loudly as if unhappy and discouraged.*)

Monkey: Hello, Anansi. Is something wrong with you?

Anansi (*Sighing again*): It's not possible. It just can't be done.

Monkey: What can't be done?

Anansi: There's a great reward for the animal who can stuff its mouth with two dozen kola nuts and still talk.

Monkey: Two dozen kola nuts? (*Pointing to tree*) Like the ones on this tree?

Anansi: Yes, and no one can do it.

Monkey: What's the reward?

Anansi: The animal who manages to stuff two dozen kola nuts into its mouth — and still talk — will become king of the forest for one week!

Monkey (*Excitedly*): Oh, oh, oh! I must have that reward!

Anansi: But no one, not even you, can do it.

Monkey: Yes I can. Just watch me.

(**Monkey** *dashes over to tree and begins stuffing kola nuts into its mouth.* **Anansi** *counts each nut the monkey stuffs into its mouth.*)

Anansi: Wonderful! Wonderful! Now talk to me.

(**Monkey** *waves hand as if trying to speak. Points to puffed cheeks, jumps up and down helplessly, and finally runs off.*)

Anansi (*Calling up to* **Nyame**): Did you see that, sky-god?

Nyame (*Laughing as before*):   Yes, Anansi. Vanity
   made the monkey quiet. I see you understand
   the ways of the world, spiderman. From this
   day on, the sky-god stories will be yours.

Storytellers   (*Together*):
   Anansi, the spiderman,
   Clever and sly.
   Though nobody fools him,
   Many still try.

QUESTIONS

A. Why do you think Nyame would not sell
   his stories?

B. What did Nyame think about Anansi at
   the end of the story?

C. What three things did Anansi have to
   show Nyame in order to get the stories?

Don't Ever Cross a Crocodile

by KAYE STARBIRD

Don't ever cross a crocodile,
However few his faults.
Don't ever dare
A dancing bear
To teach you how to waltz.

Don't ever poke a rattlesnake
Who's sleeping in the sun
And say the poke
Was just a joke
And really all in fun.

Don't ever lure a lion close
With gifts of steak and suet.
Though lion-looks
Are nice in books,
Don't ever, ever do it.

Lum Fu by HISAKO KIMISHIMA

Long ago in China, there lived a man named
Lum Fu. One night, when a huge midsummer
moon filled the sky, Lum Fu went up the mountain to gather grass for his animals. So bright was
the moon that he had no trouble finding his way
to a high mountain meadow where the grass
grew tall and sweet.

Lum Fu soon had his basket full to the top, and
he started back to his home. As he entered a
narrow pass between the high rocks, Lum Fu had
quite a surprise. A glittering path stretched before

him as far as the eye could see. Lum Fu bent
down to get a closer look. The path was covered
with gold coins shining brightly in the moonlight.

Lum Fu had barely recovered from the shock
of such a sight, when suddenly there appeared in
the middle of all the gold a strange-looking old
woman.

She smiled in a friendly way and said, "Ah!
You are a lucky man. Tonight is the full moon of
summer. Once a year at this time, the god of this
mountain spreads out his gold so that it will
gather fresh brightness from the moonlight. Because you happened to see it, I will give you
these." With that she picked up three gold coins
and gave them to the bewildered man.

Lum Fu was delighted with his good luck. After thanking the woman, he turned to continue down the mountain. Then he took one last look at the glittering gold and stopped. Three coins were very nice. But maybe if he asked her, she would give him a few more.

Going back to the old woman, he said, "Excuse me, dear grandmother. I am only a poor farmer. I have a large family. Do you suppose the mountain god would mind if you gave me a few more coins?"

Once more the woman bent down and picked up three coins. "There," she said as she handed them to him. "That should take care of you and your family." Again he thanked her and started off to his home.

This time when he looked back, the old woman had disappeared.

"All that gold," Lum Fu thought. "I'm sure the mountain god himself doesn't know how many coins there are. Here I am with only six. Surely the god wouldn't know the difference if I took a few more."

Without wasting a minute, Lum Fu emptied the grass out of his basket.

With both hands Lum Fu scooped up the gold coins and filled the basket to the very top.

But a basket filled with gold was a lot heavier than a basket filled with grass. Lum Fu soon grew tired. He came to a small stone bridge over a stream, and here he stopped to rest. As he sat there in the moonlight, he thought again of all that gold spread out on the mountain.

"How foolish I am," he said. "If I get another, larger basket, I can gather enough gold to build a palace. I will have beautiful clothes and people to wait on me. I can eat delicious food. And I will never have to work again."

Lum Fu started to hurry home for a bigger basket, but the gold on his back was so heavy that it slowed him down. "I can go faster without this," he said, throwing the basket into the stream. "Soon I will have much more gold than that." The basket made a splash as it hit the water. The gold coins sank from sight.

Once at home, he grabbed his two largest baskets. Without taking so much as a minute to rest, he started out for the mountain. But he hadn't gone too far when he stopped short.

"I am truly a fool," he laughed. "If my wife comes along, she can carry a basket of gold, too."

He hurried back home. Waking his wife, he told her about the gold coins on the mountain.

Lum Fu's wife quickly dressed while he found more baskets. Then the two set out for the mountain. They had just reached the stone bridge when Lum Fu stopped again.

"Why should we leave the grandmother and grandfather sleeping at home!" he exclaimed to his wife. "They, too, can help carry some gold. They are old and weak, but they can each carry a small basket. Even small baskets filled with gold coins will make a nice sound, and the richer we

will be." His wife agreed, grateful that she had such a clever husband.

Once more they were back at the house. Lum Fu ran about waking everyone — grandmother, grandfather, children. Soon they were all on their way up the mountain, carrying anything that would hold gold coins.

And the barnyard animals came trailing along to find out what all the fuss was about. It was quite a sight to see.

But, alas, while all this was going on, the moon had been traveling slowly, slowly across the night sky. And just as Lum Fu and his family reached the golden path, the moon slipped behind the mountain.

With a tinkling, clinking sound, the gold coins disappeared before their eyes!

Sadly they turned and started back down the mountain as the earth brightened and the morning sun rose in the eastern sky.

"Humph," the old grandmother complained.

"Why did you come back to get us? The two of you could have carried enough gold to make everyone happy."

"Or for that matter, Lum Fu," sniffed the old grandfather, "you should have been satisfied with what you could carry in your own baskets. You shouldn't have bothered to wake up your wife."

"Why didn't you just bring the first basket home?" grumbled Lum Fu's wife. "At least we would have had something to show for your night's work."

"Even the six coins the old woman gave you would have been better than nothing!" complained his son.

"And if nothing else, the three coins would have bought some rice and fish," added his daughter.

Poor Lum Fu could only hold his head and wish that he had never seen the gold coins in the moonlight. But his troubles weren't over yet.

As they crossed the stone bridge again, the animals spoke up and added their complaint.

"It would have been better if you had come back with just a basketful of grass," the animals grumbled. "Then at least we would have had something to eat for breakfast!"

QUESTIONS

A. Why do you think Lum Fu was not satisfied with the smaller amounts of gold he could have had?

B. Do you think Lum Fu will return to the same place next year to see if the gold is there? Why do you think that?

C. Do you think Lum Fu learned anything from this experience? If so, what did he learn?

A Poem from Korea

by CHUN KEUM

When darkness covers the mountain village,
A dog, far away, begins to bark.
Opening the brushwood door, I find
The night is cold and the moon is bright.

Why do you think that dog is barking
At the sleepy moon over the mountain?

VOCABULARY
The Same Words Again

Do you ever get tired of hearing the same words over and over again? Writers often use different words that mean almost the same thing to make what they write more interesting. The storytellers in "Anansi the African Spider" say that Anansi is *sly* and *clever*. Those two words mean almost the same thing. *Sly* means "clever in a sneaky way."

A story or sentence would not be very interesting if you always used the same words to mean the same thing. By using a different word, you can give the sentence more life.

Pretty is a word that is used over and over again. To make a sentence more interesting, you could use *beautiful* or *lovely*. Instead of using the word *little* all the time, you could use *small* or *tiny*. Someone could be *grouchy* or *grumpy*. A pineapple could be *tasty* or *delicious*. You could be *worried* or *anxious*.

Sometimes, in one sentence, a writer might use two different words that mean almost the same thing. In this sentence, both *awful* and *terrible* mean "very unpleasant."

He was in a *terrible, awful* mood!

The writer used both words to make sure you know just how unpleasant the person's mood was.

As you read, notice the different words a writer uses to make a story interesting. You might try to use different words as you write and talk. It will help make your ideas and sentences more fun to hear and read.

Skunk Baby

by BERNIECE FRESCHET

On a bright May morning in a hollow tree, Skunk Baby was born. He was a very curious little skunk and it wasn't long before Skunk Baby pushed out of the hollow tree. Even though he was smaller than his brother and two sisters, he was the first of the little skunks to explore the outside.

How big the world was!

The little skunk had not yet learned about enemies, and so he was not afraid. Sometimes Skunk Baby explored too far away from the safety of the tree. Then his mother would pick him up by the back of his neck and carry him home. Sometimes she would even scold him.

For a while, Skunk Baby would stay close to their den. But he loved to explore. Soon he would be off again, bravely pushing his nose into a leafy bush or under an interesting rock.

Everything was new and exciting. There was much to see and learn about in this big world. And Skunk Baby was not afraid.

As the days passed, the little skunks began to play outside more and more. The mother skunk watched over her family all the time. At the first sign of danger — a strange noise or a sudden movement — she was beside them, stamping the ground with her front feet. The young skunks knew that this was a warning to go quickly inside their den.

Skunk Baby always paid attention to his mother's warnings. But still he was not afraid.

When the young skunks were eight weeks old, the mother skunk took them on their first hunt. It was at night. Skunks hunt at night and sleep in the day.

The young skunks followed along behind their mother in a single line, their bushy tails held up high. Skunk Baby was the last in line.

The mother skunk took her family along a path at the edge of the woods. She was taking them to the pond in the meadow.

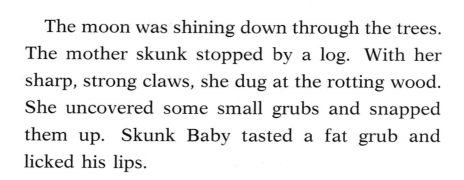

The moon was shining down through the trees. The mother skunk stopped by a log. With her sharp, strong claws, she dug at the rotting wood. She uncovered some small grubs and snapped them up. Skunk Baby tasted a fat grub and licked his lips.

Suddenly the skunks heard a strange noise at the other end of the log. A round, bristly-looking animal walked past.

The old porcupine gave a gruff warning for all to stay out of his way. He swung his bristly tail from side to side.

The mother skunk did not even look at the old porcupine. She was not afraid of him. He was not an enemy. She gave her young a sign to follow her. And off the family waddled down the path and toward the pond.

From the pond came the song of the frogs. Under rocks and leaves, crickets rubbed their wings together, making a cheerful, chirping sound.

An owl hooted!

The mother skunk stopped and listened. The owl was a dangerous enemy, but he was too far away to cause her alarm. The family continued down the path.

The frogs' singing grew louder. The skunks were almost at the pond.

Suddenly there was a soft, swishing sound overhead. The great horned owl swooped down.

The mother skunk knew that danger was near! She stamped her front feet. Her family quickly scrambled under a thorny bush.

The branches were so full of sharp thorns that it was impossible for the owl to land. Soon it hooted and flew away.

When she was sure it was safe, the mother led her family to the pond. They walked to the edge and drank the cool water.

A small, silver fish swam near. With a quick flash of her paw, the mother skunk batted the little fish out of the water and up on the shore.

Another fish swam close to Skunk Baby. He slapped the water with his front paw, as his mother had done. But it would be a while yet before he learned to bat fish out of the pond. Poor Skunk Baby rubbed the water from his eyes.

Near the pond, the mother skunk found a nest of blackbird eggs hidden in the cattails. She showed her young how to break the shells and eat the eggs. Skunk Baby licked his shell clean.

The skunks also ate seeds, leaves, grasshoppers, and mice. Then the little skunks curled up by a large rock to sleep in the warm sand.

Moonlight glittered across the pond. A big bullfrog splashed into the water. A busy beaver swam to a pile of sticks in the pond.

Skunk Baby soon grew restless. He stood up and shook the sand from his thick fur. He began to explore the edge of the pond. Soon he came upon a curious-looking toad, and he stopped to look.

In the woods nearby, a young fox moved quietly through the trees. On soft, quiet paws, he moved silently along the path.

The young fox was hungry.

At the pond, Skunk Baby put his paw on top of the curious-looking toad. In a sudden jump, the toad leaped high and hopped away. The skunk tried to follow, but the toad was soon out of sight.

Then the fox came out of the woods. He stood quietly — listening. He sniffed the warm night air. He sniffed again. He smelled something nearby.

Slowly the fox crept toward the pond. Skunk Baby had stopped to watch the hard-working beaver. The happy chirping of a cricket sounded near.

"Chug-o-rumm!" called the deep voice of the old bullfrog.

The fox was almost at the pond.

Suddenly, he saw the skunk. The fox crouched close to the ground. He had never seen a skunk before. The little fat, furry animal looked as though he would make a tasty supper.

Slowly the fox crept closer.

Closer . . . closer . . .

Now he was close enough. He crouched lower — ready to spring.

The frogs stopped their singing.

The cricket was still.

The pond grew quiet.

Slap! the beaver's tail hit the water in warning.

Skunk Baby jumped! His instinct told him that danger was near.

He saw the fox's yellow eyes and sharp pointed teeth. He heard a low growl.

For the first time in his life, Skunk Baby was afraid. He squeaked in fright. By instinct, he stamped the ground with his front feet. Then, half turning, he raised his tail high. He sprayed a strong-smelling liquid at the fox.

Suddenly his mother was beside him. She, too, sprayed the enemy, catching the fox full in the face with the liquid. Her smell was even more powerful.

The fox pawed at his burning eyes. Rolling over and over on the ground, he tried to rid himself of the smell. He ran to the pond and leaped into the water.

Tonight the young fox had learned an important lesson. And so had the little skunk.

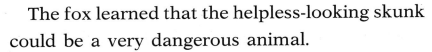

The fox learned that the helpless-looking skunk could be a very dangerous animal.

Skunk Baby learned how it felt to be afraid. Now he would remember always to be on guard for enemies. He learned something else, too. He learned that he had a very powerful weapon.

Skunk Baby was not big. He could not roar or growl. He did not have very sharp teeth. He was not a fighter.

Instead he was small and round and moved quite slowly. He looked soft and helpless.

But Skunk Baby, like all other skunks, had a weapon as powerful as that of any animal.

That night the frogs sang again.

A cricket chirped.

The black sky turned to gray and then to pink. Now the mother skunk called her little ones together. It was time to return to their den in the hollow tree.

Off the family waddled down the path, mother first, with her youngsters following along behind in a single line.

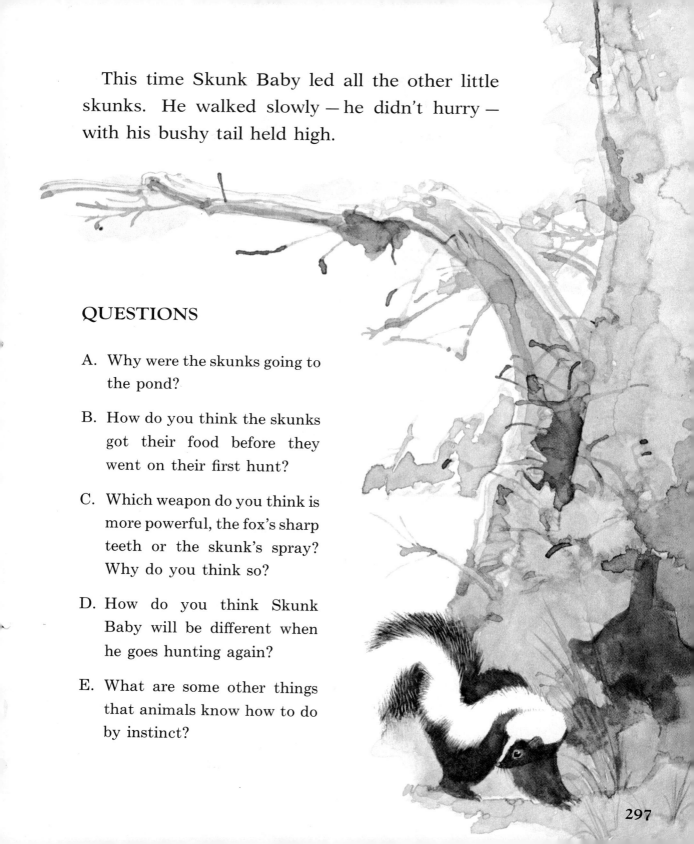

This time Skunk Baby led all the other little skunks. He walked slowly — he didn't hurry — with his bushy tail held high.

QUESTIONS

A. Why were the skunks going to the pond?

B. How do you think the skunks got their food before they went on their first hunt?

C. Which weapon do you think is more powerful, the fox's sharp teeth or the skunk's spray? Why do you think so?

D. How do you think Skunk Baby will be different when he goes hunting again?

E. What are some other things that animals know how to do by instinct?

The Sun

by NATALIA BELTING

The sun is a yellow-tipped porcupine
Lolloping through the sky,
Nibbling treetops and grasses and weeds,
Floating on rivers and ponds,
Casting shining barbed quills at the earth.

(based on the folklore of the Crow Indians)

Truth or Fantasy?

Have you ever thought about the kinds of stories that you like to read? You may like to read true stories, stories about people who really lived and things that really happened. Or you may enjoy true-to-life stories. "Maxie" is a true-to-life story. The story did not really happen, but it *could* have happened. This kind of story is called a **realistic story.**

Perhaps you like to read stories like "Lum Fu." Lum Fu is not a real person, and the story could not have happened. This kind of story is called a **fantasy.**

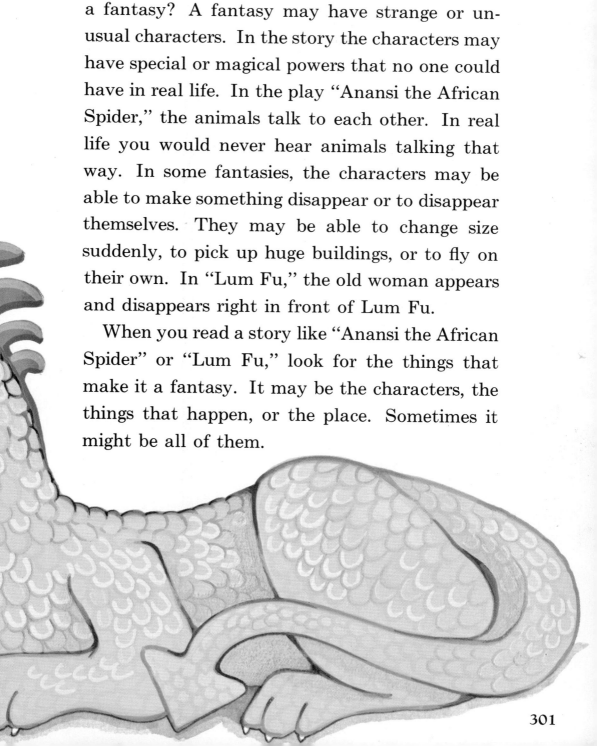

How can you tell if a story is a realistic story or a fantasy? A fantasy may have strange or unusual characters. In the story the characters may have special or magical powers that no one could have in real life. In the play "Anansi the African Spider," the animals talk to each other. In real life you would never hear animals talking that way. In some fantasies, the characters may be able to make something disappear or to disappear themselves. They may be able to change size suddenly, to pick up huge buildings, or to fly on their own. In "Lum Fu," the old woman appears and disappears right in front of Lum Fu.

When you read a story like "Anansi the African Spider" or "Lum Fu," look for the things that make it a fantasy. It may be the characters, the things that happen, or the place. Sometimes it might be all of them.

DECIDING BETWEEN TRUTH AND FANTASY

Each of the following groups of sentences tells about a story. Which ones tell about realistic stories and which ones tell about fantasy? Tell what makes the story a fantasy.

1. Two boys are camping out in the back yard. They are frightened by what looks like a ghost flying around in the darkness. Then they discover that the ghost is only a white sheet flapping in the breeze.

2. A man's ship sinks in a storm and he swims to an island. He is tired and falls asleep at once. When he wakes up, he finds himself tied to the ground. All around him are tiny men six inches tall.

3. A boy wants to be a baseball player. But he is very small for his age. So he practices baseball whenever he can. In a few years, even though he is still small, the boy becomes very strong. He later becomes one of the best baseball players in the country.

4. While she is traveling underground, a little girl finds a bottle. Tied to the bottle is a label with the words, "DRINK ME." When she does, she starts growing smaller and smaller.

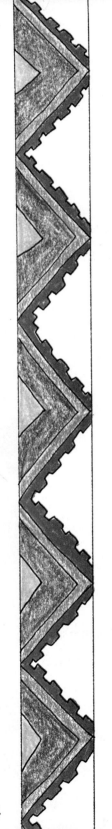

The Goat in the Rug

by GERALDINE as told to CHARLES L. BLOOD
and MARTIN LINK

My name is Geraldine and I live near a place
called Window Rock with my Navajo friend,
Glenmae. It's called Window Rock because
there is a big round hole in it that looks like a
window open to the sky.

Glenmae is called Glenmae most of the time
because it's easier to say than her Navajo name:
Glee 'Nasbah. In English that means something
like "woman warrior." But Glenmae is really a
Navajo weaver. I guess that's why, one day, she
decided to weave me into a rug.

I remember it was a warm, sunny afternoon. Glenmae had spent most of the morning sharpening a large pair of scissors. I had no idea what she was going to use them for, but it didn't take me long to find out.

Before I knew what was happening, I was on the ground. Glenmae was cutting off my wool. (It's called mohair, really.) It didn't hurt at all, but I did kick up my heels some. I'm very ticklish for a goat.

I might have looked a little bare and silly afterwards, but my, did I feel nice and cool! So I decided to stick around and see what would happen next.

The first thing Glenmae did was chop up roots from a yucca plant. The roots made a soapy, rich foam when she mixed them with water. She washed my wool in the soapy mixture until it was clean and white.

After that, a little bit of me (you might say) was hung up in the sun to dry. When my wool was dry, Glenmae took out two large combs with many teeth. These are called carding combs. By combing my wool between the carding combs, she removed any bits of twigs and straightened out the wool. She told me this helped make a smoother yarn. Then Glenmae carefully started to spin my wool into yarn. She did one small bundle at a time. I was beginning to find out it takes a long while to make a Navajo rug.

Again and again, Glenmae twisted and pulled, twisted and pulled the wool. Then she spun it around a long, thin stick. The yarn became finer, stronger, and smoother as she twisted, pulled, and spun.

A few days later, Glenmae and I went for a walk. She said we were going to find some special plants. She would use these plants to make dye.

I didn't know what "dye" meant, but it sounded like a picnic to me. I do love to eat plants. That's what got me into trouble.

While Glenmae was out looking for more plants, I ate every single one she had already collected in her bucket. Delicious!

The next day, Glenmae made me stay home while she walked miles to a store. She said the dye she could buy wasn't the same as the kind she makes from plants. But since I'd made such a pig of myself, it would have to do.

I was really worried that she would still be angry with me when she got back. She wasn't, though. Pretty soon she had three big potfuls of dye boiling over a fire.

Then I saw what Glenmae had meant by dyeing. She dipped my white wool into one pot . . . and it turned pink! She dipped it in again. It turned a darker pink! By the time she'd finished dipping it in and out and hung it up to dry, it was a beautiful deep red.

After that, she dyed some of my wool brown, and some of it black. I couldn't help wondering if those plants I'd eaten would turn me into the same colors.

While I was worrying about that, Glenmae started to make our rug. She took a ball of yarn and wrapped it around and around two poles. I lost count when she'd reached three hundred wraps. I guess I was too busy thinking about what it would be like to be the only red, white, black, and brown goat at Window Rock.

It wasn't long before Glenmae had finished wrapping. Then she hung the poles with the yarn on a big wooden frame. It looked like a picture frame made of logs. She called it a "loom."

After a whole week of getting ready, Glenmae started weaving. She began at the bottom of the loom. Then, one strand of yarn at a time, our rug started growing toward the top.

A few strands of black.

A few of brown.

A few of red.

In and out. Back and forth.

Until, in a few days, the design of our rug was clear to see.

Our rug grew very slowly. Just as every Navajo weaver before her had done for hundreds and hundreds of years, Glenmae formed a design that would never be exactly copied.

Then, at last, the weaving was finished! But I didn't let Glenmae take our rug off the loom until I'd checked it very carefully in front . . . and in back.

There was a lot of me in that rug. I wanted it to be just right. And it was.

Since then, my wool has grown almost long enough for Glenmae and me to make another rug. I hope we do very soon. Because, you see, there aren't too many weavers like Glenmae left among the Navajos.

And there is only one goat like me. Geraldine.

QUESTIONS

A. What were some of the steps Glenmae followed in making the rug?

B. How can plants be used in making a Navajo rug?

C. What did Glenmae have to use in making her rug that Navajo weavers hundreds of years ago did not use?

D. Why do you think there are only a few weavers like Glenmae left?

E. If you had a chance to learn how to make a rug, what kind of design would you weave? What colors would you choose?

Plants

by MARCI RIDLON

Prickly, shiny, leafy, viney
tall and small and thick and thin,
smooth or bumpy, single, clumpy,
some grow outside, some grow in.

Waxy, seedy, tasty, weedy,
some are pretty, some are plain.
Soft or beady, spiky, reedy,
some like dryness, some love rain.

Smelly, fluffy, rough or puffy,
in the ground or in a pot,
juicy, silky, spicy, milky,
some like cold, some like it hot.

The Rooster Who Understood Japanese

by YOSHIKO UCHIDA

"Mrs. K.!" Miyo called. "I'm here!"

Every afternoon when Miyo came home from school, she went to the home of her neighbor, Mrs. Kitamura, whom she called "Mrs. K."

This was because Miyo's mother was a doctor at University Hospital and didn't get home until supper time. Sometimes she didn't get home even then. And if she didn't, Miyo just stayed on at Mrs. K's.

It was a fine arrangement all around. Mrs. K's husband had died, and she enjoyed Miyo's company. Not that she was lonely. She had a basset hound named Jefferson, a ten-year-old parrot named Hamilton, a black cat named Leonardo, and a pet rooster named Mr. Lincoln. She talked to all of them in Japanese. She also talked to the onions and potatoes that she had planted in her front yard instead of grass. Each day she would encourage them to grow plump and delicious.

About the time Miyo came home from school, Mrs. K. was usually outside talking to her potatoes and onions. But today Mrs. K. was nowhere to be seen. She wasn't out front. And she wasn't in back talking to any of her animals either.

Her dog, Jefferson, came to meet Miyo as she opened the gate to the back yard.

"Hello, Jefferson Kitamura," she said. "Where's Mrs. K.?"

Jefferson wagged his tail and sniffed at Miyo. Then he went back to his special spot at the foot of the big tree. He curled up to get on with his afternoon nap.

Miyo stopped next to see Mr. Lincoln. He was strutting about in his pen making rooster-like sounds. He looked very proud and very intelligent. Mrs. K. had told Miyo that he understood every word she said to him, in either English or Japanese.

"Mrs. Kitamura, *doko?*" Miyo said, asking Mr. Lincoln where she was. He bent his head, looked at her with his small bright eyes, and made a squawking sound.

Miyo shrugged her shoulders. Maybe Mr. Lincoln did understand Japanese. But it certainly didn't do her any good if she couldn't understand what he said back to her.

"Never mind," she said. "I'll find her." And she hurried toward the brown house covered with ivy that hung over it like floppy hair. The back door was unlocked and Miyo walked in.

"Mrs. K.! I'm here," she called once more.

All at once a high shrill voice repeated, "Mrs. K.! I'm here." It was Hamilton, the parrot. He lived in a big gold cage in Mrs. Kitamura's kitchen.

"Hello, Hamilton," Miyo said.

"Hello, Hamilton," he answered back.

Miyo went into the dining room. She found
Mrs. K. sitting at the big dining room table.
Mrs. K. still wore her floppy gardening hat over
the pile of gray hair, and she was doing something Miyo had never seen her do before. She
was making herself a cup of ceremonial Japanese tea. She was stirring the special green tea
in a beautiful tea bowl.

Miyo knew exactly what Mrs. K. was doing.
She had seen a woman perform the Japanese tea
ceremony at the temple just last month.

"*Mah!*" Mrs. K. said, looking startled. "I was so busy with my thoughts, I didn't even hear you come in."

Miyo looked at the light green tea in the tea bowl, knowing it was strong and bitter. "Is that our afternoon tea?" she asked, trying not to look too disappointed.

"No, no, not yours," Mrs. K. answered quickly. "Just mine. I made it to calm myself." She turned the bowl around carefully, drinking it in the proper three and a half sips. "There," she sighed.

"Are you calm now?" asked Miyo.

Mrs. K. shook her head. "Not really. Actually, not at all. As a matter of fact, I am most upset."

Mrs. Kitamura stood up and started toward the kitchen. Leonardo appeared from under her chair to follow close behind. Miyo thought Leonardo was a strange name for a cat. But Mrs. K. had told her that he was a very intelligent, creative cat, and that she had named him after the Italian artist Leonardo da Vinci.

In fact, all of Mrs. K's pets had important, dignified names. They were names she had picked after going to a class in American history.

She said animals should have names that fit their characters. "Besides," she had added, "I like to be different."

Mrs. K. certainly was different, all right. Maybe it was because she had lived in America so much longer than most of the other women who had come from Japan. She never did anything she didn't want to do. Yet she was always careful not to cause anyone any trouble.

Miyo wondered now why Mrs. K. was so upset. Usually she was full of fun. But today she barely smiled at Miyo.

"I've been upset since seven o'clock this morning," she explained suddenly.

"Why?" Miyo asked, gratefully taking the milk and cookies Mrs. K. offered her. "Did you get out of the wrong side of bed?" That was what her mother sometimes asked when Miyo was grumpy. But that wasn't Mrs. K's trouble at all.

"It's not me," she said. "It's Mr. Wickett, my new neighbor. He told me that if Mr. Lincoln didn't stop waking him up by crowing at six in the morning, he would call the police. Can you imagine anything so unfriendly?"

Miyo certainly couldn't. "That's mean," she said.

"What am I going to do?" Mrs. K. asked. "I can't go out and tell Mr. Lincoln he is not to crow anymore. That would be like telling Jefferson not to wag his tail. Or telling Leonardo not to lick his fur."

"Or telling Hamilton not to repeat what we say," Miyo added.

"Exactly," Mrs. K. agreed. "Mr. Lincoln is only acting in his own rooster-like way. And besides," she added, "any respectable old man should be up by six o'clock anyway!"

Miyo wondered what she could say to make Mrs. K. feel better. Finally she said, "I'll ask my mother. She'll know what to do." Miyo's mother usually found a way to solve most problems. She had to, because Miyo had no father, and there was no one else in their house to ask. Miyo's father had died long ago, and Miyo barely remembered him.

"Don't worry. Mama will think of something," Miyo said as she left Mrs. Kitamura's house.

Mrs. K. nodded. "I hope so," she said sadly. "In the meantime, I must think of something before six o'clock tomorrow morning."

When Miyo got home, Mother was just starting supper. "Hi, sweetie," she called. "How was Mrs. K.?"

"She was worried," Miyo answered as she began to set the table. "She's got to make Mr. Lincoln stop crowing."

"Whatever for?"

Miyo quickly told Mother about Mr. Wickett. "Isn't that mean?" she said. "Mr. Lincoln doesn't hurt anybody."

But Mother said, "Well, I can see Mr. Wickett's side, too. Mr. Lincoln doesn't bother us because we're up anyway. But if I could sleep late, I'm not so sure I'd like having a rooster wake me at six o'clock. Besides," she added, "our town is growing. We're in the city limits now. Maybe Mrs. K. will just have to give Mr. Lincoln away."

Miyo didn't even want to think of such a thing. "But he's not just any old rooster," she said. "Besides, he doesn't crow very loud."

"I know," Mother agreed. "Well, maybe we can think of something."

A Home for Mr. Lincoln

That first night Mrs. K. brought Mr. Lincoln inside the house and stuffed him into a big cardboard box in her bedroom.

"Poor Mr. Lincoln," she said to Miyo the next day. "He nearly smothered. And I hardly got any sleep at all. He crowed in the morning anyway. I don't think Mr. Wickett heard him because so far the police haven't come. But I jump every time my doorbell rings. What on earth are we going to do?"

Miyo wished she had an answer. All she could say was, "Mama and I are both thinking very hard."

But Mother was so tired at the end of a long day at the hospital that she just couldn't find any good ideas inside her head. She did say, however, that keeping Mr. Lincoln inside a box in the house was not the answer.

And Mrs. K. certainly found out it wasn't. On the second night she brought him inside, Mr. Lincoln pecked his way right out of the box and walked all over the house. He scratched the floors and pecked at her chairs. He got into a fight with Leonardo, the cat. By the time Mrs. K. got to them, there were feathers all over her living room.

"I suppose I will have to give Mr. Lincoln away," Mrs. K. said sadly. "But I can't give him to just anybody. It has to be someone who will love him and not turn him into a fricassee or a stew."

Miyo thought and thought. How in the world could they find just the right person to take Mr. Lincoln? Then suddenly, Miyo had an idea.

"I know," she said brightly. "I'll put an ad in our class newspaper."

Miyo's class newspaper was almost ready for the month of October. There were sections for news, stories, sports, poems, and, at the end, a small section for ads. That's where Miyo thought Mr. Lincoln would fit nicely.

Miyo made her ad very special. She wrote, "Wanted: Nice home for friendly, intelligent, dignified rooster. P. S. He understands Japanese." Then she added, "Please hurry. Urgent."

Her teacher, Mrs. Fielding, told her it was a fine ad. She suggested that Miyo put in her phone number, so Miyo did. She also drew a picture of Mr. Lincoln beside her ad, trying to make him look dignified and friendly.

The newspaper came out on September 30. That very afternoon, a police officer rang the bell at Mrs. K's ivy-covered house.

"I've had a complaint, ma'am," he said, "about a rooster?" He seemed to think there might have been some mistake.

Mrs. K. sighed. "Come inside, officer," she said. "I've been expecting you."

Miyo was proud of her ad in the class newspaper. But no one seemed at all interested in Mr. Lincoln. Instead, many people told her how much they liked her story about Mr. Botts, the school custodian, who was retiring.

She had written, "Say good-by to the best custodian Hawthorn School ever had. Mr. Botts is retiring because he has worked a long time and is getting tired. He and Mrs. Botts are

moving to Far Creek. He is going to eat a lot and sleep a lot and maybe go fishing. So — so long, Mr. Botts. And good luck!"

On her way home, Miyo ran into Mr. Botts himself. He told her it was the first time in his life that anyone had written a story about him.

When he got home that night, he took off his shoes and sat in his favorite chair. Then he read the newspaper from cover to cover.

At the top of one page, he saw Miyo's ad about Mr. Lincoln.

"Tami," he said to Mrs. Botts, who happened to be Japanese. "How would you like to have a rooster that understands Japanese?"

"A what?"

"A rooster that understands Japanese," Mr. Botts repeated. "When we move to Far Creek, didn't you say you were going to grow vegetables and raise chickens while I go fishing?"

Mrs. Botts remembered having said something like that. "Yes, I guess I did."

"Well, how would you like a rooster, too?"

"Why, I guess I would."

"Then we might as well have one that's friendly and dignified," Mr. Botts said. And he went right to the telephone to call Miyo.

"I'll take that rooster you want to find a home for," he said. "My wife Tami could talk to it in Japanese, too."

Miyo couldn't believe it. Someone had actually read her ad, and that someone was Mr. Botts and his wife. They would give Mr. Lincoln a fine home and surely wouldn't turn him into a fricassee or a stew. At last she had done something to help Mrs. K. As soon as she told Mother, she ran right over to tell Mrs. K. the good news.

"Hooray! *Banzai!*" Mrs. K. said happily. "Tomorrow we will have a party to celebrate. I shall invite you and your mama, and Mr. and Mrs. Botts." And because Mrs. K. felt so relieved and happy, she even decided to invite Mr. Wickett.

"Even though you are a cross old man," she said to Mr. Wickett, "I suppose you were right. A rooster shouldn't live in a small pen at the edge of town. He should live in the country where he'll have some hens to talk to and nobody will care if he crows at the sun."

Mr. Wickett was a little embarrassed to come to Mrs. K's party, but he was too lonely to say no. He came with some flowers and said, "I'm sorry I made such a fuss."

Mrs. K. told him he needn't be sorry. "Life needs a little stirring up now and then," she said. "Besides," she added, "now both Mr. Lincoln and I have found new friends."

Miyo and her mother brought a cake with Mr. Lincoln's name on it, and Mr. and Mrs. Botts brought Mrs. K. a plant. "Maybe you can talk to the plant in Japanese instead of to Mr. Lincoln," Mrs. Botts said. "And don't worry. I'll take good care of Mr. Lincoln."

"You come on out to visit us and your rooster any time you like," Mr. Botts added.

Miyo's mother promised that one day soon she would drive them all up to Far Creek to see how Mr. Lincoln liked his new home.

When the party was over, Mr. Botts carried the rooster in a box to his station wagon. Mr. Lincoln gave a polite squawk of farewell, and Mrs. K. promised she would come visit him soon.

"Good-by, Mr. Lincoln. Good-by, Mr. and Mrs. Botts," Miyo called.

From inside Mrs. K's kitchen, Hamilton, the parrot, repeated, "Good-by, Mr. Lincoln. Good-by!"

Jefferson got up from his bed near the stove and came outside to wag his tail at everybody. And Leonardo rubbed up against Mrs. K's legs to remind her that he was still there.

Then Mr. Botts honked his horn and they were gone.

"I hope we'll see each other again soon," Mr. Wickett said to Mrs. K.

"Good night, Mr. Wickett," she answered. "I'm sure we will."

Miyo and her mother thanked Mrs. K. for the nice party and went home, leaving her to say good night to her potatoes and onions before going inside.

"Do you think she'll miss Mr. Lincoln a lot?" Miyo asked.

"She will for a while," Mother answered. "But now she has a new friend and neighbor to talk to."

Miyo nodded. That was true. She was glad everything turned out so well. She went to bed feeling good inside.

"Good night, Mama," she called softly to her mother.

"Good night, Miyo," Mother answered as she tucked her in.

Then, one by one, the lights went out in all the houses along the street, and soon only the sounds of the crickets filled the dark night air.

QUESTIONS

A. Mr. Wickett and Mrs. K. disagreed about the rooster. What was Mrs. K.'s side of the argument? What was Mr. Wickett's side of the argument with Mrs. K.?

B. Would you have agreed with Mr. Wickett or Mrs. K. about the rooster? Explain your answer.

C. Why was Mr. Botts able to give the rooster a good home?

D. What good thing happened to Mrs. K. because of this problem?

THE HAWTHORN SCHOOL NEWS

MR. BOTTS RETIRES

Say good—by to the best custodian Hawthorn School ever had. Mr. Botts is retiring because he has worked a long time and is getting tired. He and Mrs. Botts are moving to Far Creek. He is going to eat a lot and sleep a lot and maybe go fishing. So—so long, Mr. Botts. And good luck!

GATSBY THE GREAT COMES TO HAWTHORN SCHOOL

Gatsby the Great came to our school last month. She performed many tricks.

Everyone's favorite trick was the Disappearing Homework Trick. Gatsby copied down some words on a paper. When she showed it to us, the words had disappeared! Then she held the paper near a light and—presto—the words appeared!

Before she left, Gatsby told us her secret. She wrote the words with milk!

Hawthorn School Wins!

Hawthorn School's best runners raced with runners from Park Street School. Hawthorn School won every race!

Jane Wong and Lisa West tied for first place in the longest race. Jeff Marks won two races.

☆ Jokes & Riddles ☆

Where does February come before January?

in a dictionary

Jim: What's the name of your dog?
Kim: Ginger.
Jim: Does Ginger bite?
Kim: No, Ginger snaps!

·ADS·

The Wizard's Tears

by MAXINE KUMIN and ANNE SEXTON

Everything was going wrong in the town of
Drocknock. All summer there had been a
drought. The reservoir was drying up. Twenty
cows had disappeared from Farmer Macadoo's
meadow without a trace. And worst of all, the old
wizard's spells no longer worked. He could not
for the life of him bring rain or find the cows.
Moreover, all the people of Drocknock had the
chicken pox, and the old wizard could not cure
them. Even the Mayor of Drocknock was covered
with itchy red bumps.

"It's no use," the old wizard said sadly to the mayor. "My abracadabras are all worn out. And my crystal ball is a disgrace. It's covered with black and white spots like your old dog. And speaking of old dogs, I wish he wouldn't smile at me all the time. I think he thinks I'm a joke."

"See here," said the mayor, twisting the key to the city on the ribbon around her neck. "Drocknock needs you. We can't get along without a wizard. And we can't get along without a smiling dog, either. Wise dogs smile, you know."

The water commissioner took off his red hunting cap to scratch some of his chicken pox. "I agree," he said. "We need a wizard for our drought."

"Don't worry," said the old wizard. "I've sent for a replacement. As soon as the new wizard gets here, I'll tell him all the town troubles. Then I'm moving into the Home for Retired Wizards."

The new wizard appeared that very afternoon on a red motor bike. He was very young and nervous. He had never been away from home before, and he was lonely already.

"First we must get after the itches," he said bravely, for he was not sure how. But under *Chicken Pox* in the Wizard Encyclopedia, he read the proper spell for curing red bumps:

WATCH THE MOON OVER YOUR SHOULDER. CATCH A BEE IN A JAR. AND WASH YOUR FACE WITH BUTTERMILK.

The mayor called a town meeting. The young wizard timidly gave the directions.

"How clever," said the townspeople. "The old wizard never did anything but repeat abracadabra." And they looked at the moon over their left shoulders. Each one caught a bee in a jar. And they all washed their faces with buttermilk. That was the end of the chicken pox.

The young wizard was a great success. The people of Drocknock carried him around the town on their shoulders.

"Thank you! Thank you!" he said. "I love you all. I will be the wisest wizard you ever had."

Next he looked up *Cows, disappearing,* in the Wizard Encyclopedia. It said this:

CUT ONE FINGERNAIL AND BURY IT. EAT FIVE PEAS WITH A KNIFE. SAY THE NAMES OF ALL YOUR COWS BACKWARDS.

Farmer Macadoo did as he was told. He had hardly finished saying the last three names — Sseb, Yam, and Nna — when the missing cows came in a single line down the hill into the barn.

"Hot ziggity," said the farmer. "What a wonderful young wizard you are." And he gave a big dance in the barnyard that very night to celebrate the return of his cows.

But the mayor took the young wizard aside. "See here," she said. "The drought is our most important problem. We can't wash our clothes or water our gardens anymore."

"I agree," said the water commissioner. "We're all thirsty. There is no relief. Nobody can have more than one cup of water a day, and soon that will be gone."

"A drought is hard," the young wizard said uncertainly. And he went home to look for the answer in the Wizard Encyclopedia. There was nothing under *Droughts.* He looked under *Wells, dry; Reservoirs;* and then under *Rain, How to Make.* There he found the answer:

BLOW UP ONE HUNDRED BALLOONS. HANG THEM FROM ONE HUNDRED OWLS' NESTS. COOK ONE THOUSAND AND ONE DAISIES AND EAT THEM AT HIGH

NOON. SPRINKLE THE EMPTY RESERVOIR WITH FIVE WIZARD'S TEARS. And then, written in large red letters, WARNING: PROCEED WITH CARE.

The mayor and the water commissioner and the wizard blew up balloons until their cheeks were stretched out of shape. The people of Drocknock shook their heads. "Daisies!" they grumbled. "No one eats daisies." But pick them they did. And eat them they did, cooked in lemon juice and butter.

It was not so easy for the wizard, however. He sat by the reservoir and thought sad thoughts, but the tears would not come.

"I have a problem," he said. "Drocknock has made me too happy. How can I cry when everyone here loves me?"

He went home and dialed the old wizard. "Old wizard, I am in trouble. I am so happy, I cannot cry the tears needed to end the drought."

Now the old wizard was wise in the ways of living, even though his abracadabras had worn out. "Peel an onion," he suggested. "And the tears will come. But *beware, beware*. Don't overdo it. A wizard's tears are precious. A wizard's tears are powerful. They can make strange magic."

The young wizard peeled an onion and cried ten tears into a teacup. Five of these he sprinkled into the empty reservoir. And the rains came just as the old wizard had promised. It rained for five days and five nights. The umbrella shop did a big business. The reservoir filled and there was water for everyone.

The townspeople were so grateful that they gave a roller-skating party in honor of the young wizard. The band played the Skater's Waltz and everyone whizzed around in pairs.

Beware! Beware!

The next morning the young wizard looked at the five tears left in the teacup by his bed. He forgot the old wizard's warning. "Powerful tears, what can you do for me?" he asked. "Can you bring me my breakfast in bed?"

He dipped in his finger and blew the tears one by one into the air. *Beware, beware!* sang in his head, but he paid no attention. All at once, a magnificent breakfast appeared. There were pancakes, scrambled eggs, orange juice, coffee, and a piece of chocolate cake. The tears even knew he loved chocolate cake.

It was such a magnificent breakfast that the wizard decided he would order one every morning. That night he peeled an onion and tucked it under his pillow.

"When I wake up tomorrow," he thought, "I will cry into the teacup and order another fine breakfast."

But the wizard had a restless night. Every time he turned on his pillow, the smell of the onion tickled his nose and tears ran down his cheeks in his sleep. By morning the bed was as wet as a bathmat. But although the wizard closed his eyes and pressed his fingers to his temples, the breakfast did not appear.

"Oh, dear," he wondered. "What have I done with my precious wizard's tears? Have I used up my magic? Why didn't I listen to the warnings, *beware, beware?* Maybe the old wizard can tell me." And he hurried out to the red motor bike.

On the way to the old wizard's, he met the big yellow school bus. It was stopped in the middle of the road. Frogs peered out at him from every window.

"What's going on here?" he asked himself. But there was no one to answer. Inside his head a little voice repeated, *beware, beware!*

At the next corner the wizard pulled into the gas station. In the doorway there sat a large green frog. There was no one to fill his gas tank. *Beware, beware.*

Fearing the worst, he hurried off to the mayor's house to tell her the strange happenings.

In the mayor's kitchen, two frogs sat on the table. One wore the key to the city around its neck. The other peeked out from the water commissioner's red hunting cap. "Croak, croak!" they said as he entered.

"Oh, dear! What have I done to Drocknock?" cried the young wizard. "Have I bewitched the whole town with my tears?" He put the two frogs in his pocket to keep them safe and ran out into the street for help.

But every house and shop held nothing but frogs. There was no one left in the town of Drocknock but the mayor's old dog.

The young wizard walked up and down the frog-filled streets. How lonely he was! There was no one to talk to.

"I must hurry to the old wizard," he said. "Maybe he has an abracadabra. Maybe he can help me undo what I have done."

"Look what happened," he said to the old wizard. He took the two frogs out of his pocket. "This is the mayor. And this is the water commissioner."

"I told you *beware*. Wizard's tears are precious. Wizard's tears are powerful. They must never be used for breakfast in bed," said the old wizard when he had heard the sad story.

"And I was so happy in Drocknock," said the young wizard.

The old wizard took pity on him. "I will give you a riddle," he said. "Guess the answer to this riddle and your town will fill up with people again. What is white with black spots in the daytime and black with white spots at night? The answer is under your nose. Guess the answer in three days, and Drocknock will be itself again."

The young wizard hurried back to town. He took the mayor and the water commissioner out of his pocket and set them down very gently at the edge of the reservoir. He didn't know the answer to the riddle yet. But he did know that frogs needed water.

All afternoon he went from house to house, collecting frogs and stacking them in his wheelbarrow. He carried them to the reservoir and put them carefully, one by one, at the water's edge. They all croaked and jumped into the mud. As he worked, the young wizard repeated the riddle. "What is white with black spots in the daytime and black with white spots at night?"

"I have it!" He hurried to the phone. "Old Wizard, I have it! The answer is a newspaper."

"No," said the old wizard. "That's not it. The answer is right under your nose." And he hung up with a click.

"Oh, I'm so lonely," said the young wizard. "If only there were someone to talk to. The mayor is a wise woman. She would help me think of the answer to the riddle. But now she is only a frog." And he was so sad that he cried some real tears. Presto! There was a magnificent breakfast before him, complete with chocolate cake. But he was too sad to eat. He fed the cake to the dog, who wagged his tail and smiled.

The next day the young wizard woke up with a new guess in his head. He hurried to call the old wizard. "I have it!" he said. "The answer is a birch tree."

"No," said the old wizard. "That's not it. The answer is right under your nose."

The young wizard spent another lonely day. At the reservoir the frogs croaked in chorus.

The next morning he had another guess. "A blueberry muffin!" he cried to the old wizard. And again the old wizard said, "No. That's not it. The answer is right under your nose. You have until sunset to save Drocknock." And again the phone went click.

Sadly the young wizard walked down to the reservoir once more. He sat on a log and listened to the frogs, and the old dog sat at his feet. They sat silently all day, a miserable pair. The sun was beginning to go down in the afternoon sky. The wizard tried to keep from crying, but the true tears came thick and fast. And with them came breakfast after breakfast, carefully stacked at the water's edge. Even the old dog was sad and did not beg for chocolate cake.

"I'm not much of a wizard," he said to the dog. "I can't even guess the answer to a riddle. Here you are, just an old spotted dog, but I bet you could do better than I can. You with all your black spots. Come to think of it, you look like a newspaper. Come to think of it, you look like a birch tree. Come to think of it, you even look like a blueberry muffin! That's it! That's it! What is white with black spots in the daytime and black with white spots at night? A Dalmatian dog is! A spotted Dalmatian dog!"

And before his very eyes the frog with the key around its neck turned back into the mayor. The frog with the red hunting cap turned back into the water commissioner. The gas station woman and

Farmer Macadoo and all the townspeople came out of the water in their old shapes.

"See here," said the mayor, after the young wizard had told her the whole story. "That will be enough of that. No more breakfasts in bed for you. No more onions under the pillow."

"I'm starved," said the water commissioner. "I think I will eat this breakfast."

"Me, too," said Farmer Macadoo. And they all gathered around to eat.

"Chocolate cake," said the mayor. "That's my favorite breakfast." And she forgave the young wizard his foolish tears.

And the mayor's dog smiled his old smile.

QUESTIONS

A. Why do you think the young wizard kept asking the old wizard for help?

B. Why do you think the wizard's tears worked to end the drought but did not work to get breakfast in bed every day?

C. Why do you think the young wizard did not pay attention to the old wizard's warning?

D. Do you think the young wizard will act differently if the old wizard gives him another warning? Why or why not?

E. Do you think the people of Drocknock will want the new wizard to stay? Why or why not?

F. What could the townspeople have done to solve their problems if they hadn't had a wizard?

Books to Enjoy

Why Mosquitoes Buzz in People's Ears
by Verna Aardema

In this African folk tale, a mosquito tells a story
that causes trouble. A Caldecott Medal Winner.

The Great Green Turkey Creek Monster
by James Flora

In this crazy tall tale, an enormous green vine grows
and grows, tying up the whole town.

Bear Mouse by Berniece Freschet

A meadow mouse faces many dangers every day.

Jenny and the Tennis Nut by Janet Schulman

Jenny shows her father she's good at her own
game — but it's not tennis.

I Was All Thumbs by Bernard Waber

An octopus has always lived in a tank. When he is
taken out to sea, he has quite an adventure.

Glossary

This glossary can help you find out meanings of words in this book that you may not know. The meanings of the words as they are used in this book are always given. Often you will also find other common meanings listed.

A

actually   Really; in fact.

ajar   Partly open.

alarm   A sudden warning.

alas   A word used to show sadness.

amusement park   A park that has many kinds of rides and games.

anxiously   In a worried, uneasy way.

appreciate   To know the importance of; to enjoy and understand: *She appreciates good stories and poems.*

argue   1. To fight or disagree. 2. To give reasons for or against something.

arrangement   1. An agreement: *We had an arrangement to share the work.*   2. A plan or preparation: *We made arrangements to go to camp.*

B

baggage   The trunks, bags, or suitcases in which a person carries things while traveling.

basset hound   A kind of dog with long, droopy ears and short legs.

bent   1. Curved or crooked: *The nail was bent.*   2. A readiness to act in a certain way: *She seems to have a bent for making friends.*

beware   To watch out for; to be on guard.

bewildered   Puzzled; confused.

bitter   1. Sharp or unpleasant tasting: *The lemon was bitter.*   2. Sharp or painful to the body or mind: *It was a bitter wind.*

boom   To say or speak in a loud, deep voice.

bristly   Having straight, stiff hairs.

C

calm 1. Peaceful and quiet; not excited. 2. To make peaceful and quiet.

camera A special machine used to take photographs: *With his new camera, Mark took a picture of his dog.*

canary 1. A yellow songbird that many people keep as a pet. 2. A bright yellow color.

carding comb A wire brush used to comb out and untangle wool before it is spun.

catalog A book that lists things for sale. It may have pictures and descriptions of those things.

celebrate To mark a special day with happy, joyous activities: *They celebrated her birthday by having a party.*

ceremony A special act performed in honor or celebration of something: *Everyone came to the wedding ceremony.*

certainly Surely; without question or doubt.

character 1. A person or animal in a play or story. 2. All the traits or qualities that make up someone or something.

chat 1. A friendly, relaxed talk or conversation. 2. A North American songbird with a yellow breast.

chorus Something said or sung by many people at one time. — **in chorus.** All together.

claw A sharp, sometimes curled, nail on the toe of an animal.

commissioner A person in charge of a special department: *He is the town police commissioner.*

company 1. Companionship or friendship. 2. A guest or visitor. 3. A business.

complain To say something in an unhappy, dissatisfied, or displeased way: *She complained about the weather.*

complete 1. To finish something. 2. Fully furnished or equipped: *The model kit came complete with directions.*

contents Anything that is inside a box, basket, or any other kind of container: *They emptied the contents of the jar.*

continue To keep on doing or saying something.

conversation A relaxed, familiar talk between people.

creature A living thing, especially an animal.

crouch To get down close to the ground by bending or squatting.

cure To make someone well or better.

curious Eager to learn about something.

custodian A person who takes care of a building.

D

Dalmatian A kind of dog with short white hair and many black spots.

delicious Very good tasting or smelling.

den 1. A shelter for wild animals. 2. A small room for studying or relaxing.

design An arrangement of shapes, lines, colors, or pictures into a special pattern.

determined Being very firm; decided: *He was determined to be first in line.*

dignified Having honor, importance, and respect.

diner 1. A restaurant that is shaped like a train car. 2. A person eating a meal.

disappoint To fail to fulfill some wish or hope: *He disappointed his friends by not coming to the party.*

disgraceful Shameful or dishonorable: *The mean way she acted toward her sister was disgraceful.*

dissatisfaction The feeling of being displeased; unhappy or not satisfied with something.

dozen A group of twelve.

drought A long stretch of time in which no rain has fallen: *The drought lasted so long that the ponds dried up.*

dye Anything used to color or change the color of things such as hair or cloth.

E

earthquake A shaking of the earth caused by sudden movements underground.

embarrassed Made to feel uneasy, uncomfortable, or foolish.

emergency Something that happens suddenly and calls for quick action: *The doctor was called to the hospital to help in an emergency.*

encyclopedia A book or set of books giving information about many things. These things are listed in alphabetical order.

enemy A person, animal, or thing that may be harmful or very unfriendly.

enter 1. To come into. 2. To come out on the stage.

evict To put out; to order to leave from somewhere: *They evicted the family from their home.*

exactly 1. Just right: *This is exactly what I want.* 2. Completely correct; without mistake: *The time is exactly 8:00 P.M.*

exclaim To cry out or shout suddenly, as if surprised.

expect To look forward to something; to think that something will happen.

explore To travel through an unfamiliar place in order to learn about that place.

F

fantasy A story that could not really happen; a make-believe story.

fever A sickness in which a person has a high temperature.

flame The bright, burning part of a fire.

flight 1. The act of flying. 2. A planned airplane trip. 3. A group of stairs usually between floors in a building.

foam A mass of tiny bubbles: *When the big wave crashed against the shore, the water was white with foam.*

fricassee Pieces of chicken boiled very slowly and served in a thick gravy.

G

gaze To stare.

glitter To shine brightly; to sparkle: *The moonlight glittered on the water.*

gorgeous Very beautiful.

gourd A fruit from a vine, somewhat like a squash, with a hard outer shell. The dried, hollowed-out shell of a gourd is sometimes used as a bowl or container.

grateful Thankful.

grub A worm-like larva of some beetles and other insects.

grumble To complain in a low, grouchy voice.

grumpy Grouchy; unpleasant; cross.

H

harvest The act of picking and gathering grains, fruits, or vegetables on a farm.

hay fever An itching and reddening of the nose, eyes, or throat caused by an allergy to the pollen of certain plants.

honor To think very highly of; to have great respect for.

I

imagine To form a picture or idea in the mind: *He tried to imagine what the animal looked like.*

improve To make or do better: *We improved our playing by practicing every day.*

instinct A skill, drive, or feeling that is not learned but comes naturally: *A bird knows by instinct how to build a nest.*

intelligent 1. Wise; very smart. 2. Being able to learn, think, and understand.

ivy A hanging or climbing plant with green leaves.

K

knead To press, fold, and push into something: *We kneaded the pizza dough to make it smooth.*

L

lantern A cover for a light with glass or paper sides to let the light shine through.

limit The edge or boundary around a certain place.

liquid Any matter that is flowing and watery such as milk or juice: *Pour the liquid into the bowl.*

loom A frame or machine on which threads or yarn are woven into cloth.

M

magnificent Wonderful; grand; outstanding.

manage To succeed in doing something; to accomplish something: *We finally managed to get our chores done.*

marshal   A city official who enforces or carries out court orders.

mayor   The head of a city or town.

miserable   Very unhappy.

mistake   An action, idea, or answer that is wrong: *When he added the numbers, he made a mistake.*

mohair   The soft, silky hair of an Angora goat.

moment   A very short time.

mood   The way in which a person is feeling: *Joan was in a bad mood because she lost the game.*

moose   A large animal with wide antlers, related to the deer.

N

narrow   Not wide: *The street was too narrow for a truck to pass through.*

neighborhood   A small part or section of a city or town where people live.

nervous   Uneasy; worried; anxious.

nursery school   A school for very young children.

O

operator   Someone who runs a machine: *The telephone operator will help you make the call.*

P

parrot   A kind of bird that usually has a hooked beak and brightly colored feathers. Some kinds of parrots are kept as pets and taught to repeat words.

perfectly   1. Completely; wholly: *She is perfectly happy with her old bike.* 2. In a way that is without mistake.

perform   To act in a certain way: *She performed a special dance for us.*

pierce   To make a hole or opening.

pity   A feeling of sadness for another person's pain or unhappiness.

plump   Round and full.

porcupine   An animal that has long sharp points, called quills, on its back and sides.

precious   1. Very dear or important. 2. Highly priced; very valuable.

proceed To go onward; to continue.

promptly Acting right away; immediately.

proper Correct; appropriate; fitting.

purpose The reason, aim, or goal for doing or saying something. — **on purpose.** Not by accident; knowingly or willfully.

reservoir A lake or pond used to keep the water supply.

respectable Proper in actions, appearance, or speech: *She always behaved in a respectable manner.*

reward Something given for a special act, work, or deed: *He was given a reward for finding the lost dog.*

R

realistic Showing facts and things as they really are.

reason A purpose for acting or thinking in a certain way: *What is your reason for being late?*

relief A feeling of gladness that a problem has been solved or a pain has been removed: *It was a relief to be home safe again.*

remind To cause someone to remember something.

replacement Something or someone that takes the place of something or someone else.

reporter A person who collects facts and information for news stories: *She was a reporter for the newspaper.*

S

scatter To sprinkle around: *Scatter the seeds over the ground.*

shelter Something that gives protection or cover: *We found shelter under a tree.*

shrill High and piercing in sound: *The cry was so shrill that it seemed to hurt our ears.*

shrug To raise the shoulders to show that one is unsure, uncaring, or unfeeling.

sly Clever in a sneaky way.

smother To get too little air; to be unable to breathe.

spray To shoot out a liquid such as water: *Spray a little water on the plants.*

squash 1. A game with a ball and a racket that is played on a court with high walls around it. 2. To crush or flatten: *If you step on that tomato, you will squash it.*

stalk 1. To walk in a stiff proud manner. 2. To walk quietly so as to sneak up on something.

startled Suddenly alarmed or surprised.

strand A single thread or string.

stroll A slow, pleasant walk.

strut To walk in a stiff, proud, self-important way.

success Someone who has become rich or famous because of some actions.

suggest To offer an idea for thought or action: *I suggest that you get some rest.*

superintendent A person who is in charge of something, especially a building.

swiftly Quickly; in a very fast way.

T

tarpaulin A waterproof covering used to protect things.

thorny Full of sharp points, called thorns.

timidly In a fearful or frightened way.

torch A flame of fire burning at the top of a long stick, usually used to give light: *He carried the torch into the dark cave.*

tower 1. To rise to a great height. 2. A tall, thin building or part of a building that stands high in the air.

trace 1. Some sign showing that someone or something had been there: *We looked for some trace of the lost dog.* 2. To copy over something by following the lines.

turkey A large bird with brown feathers and a bare head and neck. It is often raised for food.

U

unpleasant Not pleasing; not nice.

urgent Calling for quick action: *Her call for help sounded urgent.*

V

vanity Too much pride; thinking too highly of oneself.

W

warrior A fighter, especially one who fights in a battle or war.

wealthy Very rich.

weapon Anything used to protect oneself from danger or harm.

weave To make cloth on a loom by placing strands of yarn or thread over and under one another.

wheelbarrow A cart with a wheel at one end and two handles at the other end, used to carry things.

wool The soft, often curly, hair of sheep and other animals, used to make yarn or cloth.

Y

yarn 1. Wool that has been twisted and spun into strands to be used for weaving. 2. A tall tale; an adventure story that is often make-believe.

yucca A plant that grows in dry places in North America. It has sharp pointed leaves and white flowers.

Reading Helps

Here are some things to remember when you meet a new word.

1. When you see a new word, think about the sounds the letters stand for. You already know the sounds the consonants and vowels stand for. Be sure the new word makes sense in the sentence.

• When you meet a word with the beginning syllable *a, be, re,* or *ex,* think about the sounds those letters stand for in words like *around, beside, remember,* and *except.*

> Are you **asleep** or **awake?**
> My house is **beyond** that hill.
> I cannot **recall** his name.
> Would you like to **explore** a new land?

2. Some words may seem new at first. But you may already know the parts that make up that word.

Pearl and Squirrel are thankful to have a new family and their own place to belong.

Next, they sit down for a
tasty holiday dinner made
just for them.

"You know," says Stan, "I have plenty of room here
if you'd like to stay and live with me."
Pearl and Squirrel jump up and give him a big hug.

"I'll take that as a yes," Stan
says with a laugh.

Stan helps them get clean and dry.

"I'm thankful for soap," Squirrel says.

"I'm thankful for towels!" Pearl shouts.

Pearl jumps into Stan's arms and Squirrel cuddles into his shirt pocket.

. . . Stan!

"There you are! I've been looking all over for you two," he says with a smile. "I thought you might be cold on a night like this. Want to join me for a nice Thanksgiving dinner?"

Shivering in the cold, the two suddenly
hear footsteps getting closer. They look out to see . . .

Pearl and Squirrel cuddle together and try to stay dry.
But soon, the soggy box is breaking apart.

"You know what, Pearl?" Squirrel asks. "You're my best friend.
No matter where we live, I'm most thankful for you."
Pearl smiles wide. "Squirrel! You're doing Thanksgiving!"

When they get back home, their box is already soaked.
Pearl curls up in the driest corner.
"I don't feel very thankful anymore," she says quietly.

The streets are cold and wet. Pearl and Squirrel shiver in the damp air.
For the first time that day, Pearl feels sad.
She wishes they had a real home.
"I'd be thankful to live here. Nice and warm, with hot food each day,"
Pearl says with a sigh.

CRACK!

They wake to rain pouring from the sky.
Pearl watches as people take their pets and leave the park in a hurry.
"We better get home!" Squirrel shouts.

"I'm thankful for this cuddly nap spot,"
Pearl says sleepily. Squirrel just nods.

They reach the meadow.
"I'm thankful for new friends," Pearl calls.
"I'd rather sit," Squirrel says.

At last, they enter the park.
"I'm thankful for this fountain to swim in!" says Pearl.
"Yuck, it looks dirty," Squirrel replies.

They walk through playgrounds.
"I'm thankful for jump rope!" Pearl yells.

They walk through yards.
"I'm thankful for fetch!" Pearl calls.

"Hey, Squirrel, let's try Thanksgiving!
We can point out all the things we're thankful for!" Pearl says.
Squirrel responds with a shrug.

Pearl wonders what Thanksgiving is.
"Thanksgiving is when you share what you're thankful for
with family and friends," Stan explains.
"I'm always thankful to spend time with you two."
Pearl gives Stan a goodbye lick before they continue to the park.

"A special treat for Thanksgiving."

Squirrel eats slowly.

Pearl does not.

They see Stan, the food cart man.
He's always kind and happy to share.
"There you are!" he calls. "I have something for you."

Squirrel would like to eat something fancy.

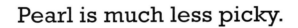

Pearl is much less picky.

They head out to the park, looking for something tasty to eat.

One morning, Pearl wakes up extra hungry.
"Get up, Squirrel!" she shouts.
"Just a few more minutes!" groans Squirrel.
Pearl nudges him. "C'mon, I'm hungry!"

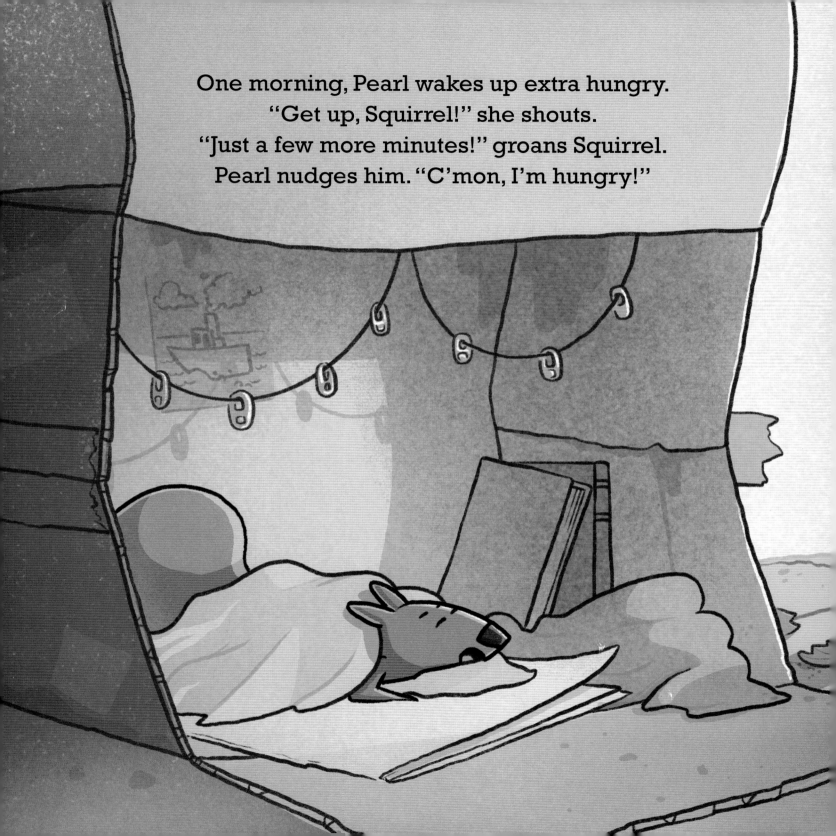

Together, they roam the city looking for adventure.

Pearl loves to play.
Her favorite place is the park.
That's where she met her best buddy, Squirrel.

Squirrel can be shy, but he's very smart.
He likes to read and learn new things.

Inside a box beside the old corner store live Pearl and Squirrel.

Library of Congress Cataloging-in-Publication Data available

ISBN 978-1-338-59209-2

10 9 8 7 6 5 4 3 2 1   20 21 22 23 24

Printed in Malaysia 108
First edition, September 2020
Book design by Rae Crawford

PEARL AND SQUIRREL GIVE THANKS

By Cassie and Ryan Ehrenberg

Orchard Books
New York
An Imprint of Scholastic Inc.